I0534705

DARKNESS DECEIVING

Origins of Morgana Le Fay
Book Two

Jen Pretty

No matter how proud you are, always remember: with the right storytelling, you will always be the villain in someone else's movie.

—UNKNOWN

CHAPTER ONE

"I remember you." My voice shook.

"I'm glad. I would hate to think I'm so forgettable." Merlin smirked. The rough stubble on his face made him look travel-worn. "You look quite different from last I saw you."

I scoffed. The heat at my back shifted, and I turned to look into the eyes of my oldest friend. "Copper," I whispered, running my hand up his forehead. He pressed against me and snuffled in my side before unfolding his forelegs and rising, shaking the snow from his woolly coat. He nickered and a horse in the distance called back.

Merlin sent out a low whistle, and the horse called back again.

The sun shone, glittering off the snow as a white mare came thundering up and slid to a halt beside us. She reached out her nose and gave an angry little huff to Copper before standing quietly beside her owner.

Merlin rose and stroked her neck.

She was beautiful but I couldn't focus on the horse as my mind swirled a million images and people who I didn't know. Thoughts jumbled, and I began to panic, my chest rising and falling fast as more and more images swirled, vying for my attention.

Merlin must have seen the terrified look on my face because magic laced his next words. "Go back to the beginning, Morgana. Put the past in order in your mind."

I pushed through the swamp of memories to one from the most important day of my life. I was eight, nearly nine years old. My father had died, and my mother remarried to a man I didn't like.

Ten years earlier.

"Morgana, those horses won't feed themselves!" Uther, my stepfather, screamed, rousing me suddenly from my sleep. I scrambled out of my bed and out of the room I shared with my sisters.

My legs carried me stumbling down the steep stairs at the back of the castle and out into the vast yard that separated the living quarters from the stable. I stumbled over a root but maintained my balance and pushed open the heavy door, letting the fresh scent of the horses and warm, humid air fill my lungs.

"Hello, darlings," I said after ensuring no one was around. If my stepfather found out I loved that job, he would surely find another for me. One I would despise.

We had several horses in the stable now, since a few knights were visiting from the south. I grabbed two buckets and carried them out of the castle ground, toward the river. It wasn't far, but it was far enough on short legs. I was strong for my age but had to make several trips twice a day to water the horses.

On my way back I glanced up and caught sight of my oldest sister. She was standing by the window of our room and appeared to be crying. I stopped for a moment, but she never looked down. She just turned away and disappeared back inside.

I would get in trouble if I didn't finish my chores, so I carried on, lugging heavy buckets until all the horses had drunk their fill and I topped up their buckets. Then I went about throwing down hay from the loft. The long metal pitchfork was difficult for me to wield. An adult man would have completed the task in minutes, but I wasn't an adult man.

I eventually gave up on the fork as I usually did and carried the hay to each stall in my arms. The coarse and prickly hay stuck in my skin, but it sped up the process.

By the time I finished feeding and watering the horses, the sun was well up. I crossed the courtyard and re-entered the castle, smelling strongly of horses and manure, although I had yet to clean the stalls. I usually let the horses eat for a while before disturbing them to do that. The break also gave me time to have breakfast. But this morning I wanted to go check on my sister. She was much older than I and often saw me as a bother, but if something upset her, I thought perhaps I could help.

I said good morning to the cooks in the kitchen, already frying eggs and pig belly and climbed the steep stairs to our room.

"Anna?" I said as I slipped through the door.

"Go away, Morgana. I've much to do." She was filling a trunk with some clothes and things.

"What are you doing?"

"I'm to be married. Now go away," she replied.

I stepped back towards the door, but it swung open and my youngest sister stepped through.

"Isn't it great?" she said, her small hands waving about. She was barely six years old but was a perpetual dreamer. Her round eyes gazed up at me with excitement.

"Lord Pendragon has found a knight to marry Anna. Do you think he will find a knight for you and me?"

A chill ran down my spine. "I don't know, Elaine." A couple of servants arrived at the room and each took an end of the trunk that Anna had filled, carrying it out of the room.

Anna went to pass us by, but I caught her arm. "Will we see you again?" I asked.

A tear slipped over Anna's eyelid to trail down her cheek. She reached down and scooped us both into her arms. I felt her body shake as though she was sobbing, but when she looked up, she wiped her tears and smiled. "I'm sure we will meet again. Be good for momma and do your chores, both of you."

Then she rose and swept out of the room, leaving us behind.

My younger sister's eyes had filled with tears as well. "I didn't know she would leave," she said on a sob.

I wrapped little Elaine up in my arms and carried her to her bed. We cuddled until her tears stopped. Then we made our way down to the kitchen and had some breakfast. Elaine was in charge of the lambs, so she had work to do as much as I.

We left the kitchen to complete our chores, my mind still on Anna and where she would end up.

A knight could travel a long distance before finally settling on a home. I knew that much.

The stable had three fewer horses when I returned to clean the stalls.

I was glad that I had at least been able to ensure Anna's horse was well fed and watered before she left. It seemed like a small consolation.

By afternoon, the stable was as spotless as Uther demanded. I was preparing to head back to the house but was surprised to see my mother open the stable door and slip inside. It was not an easy thing for her to do in her condition. Her stomach had grown so large, she struggled to walk and had been bedridden for weeks.

"Mother. What are you doing down here?" I asked, hurrying to her side. I had seen ewes give birth but seeing my mother pregnant was new.

"This baby is coming today, Morgana," she said, her voice hurried. "If it's a boy, there is a knight who will take you away. You are too young to marry. I need you to be strong, Morgana. You must run. Do you hear me?" She gripped my arm tight and I knew she was serious.

"Yes, mother."

She licked her lips and a look of pain washed over her face.

"Are you all right?" I asked.

After another moment, her face went soft, and she smiled down at me. "I will be fine as long as you are. You have a big future ahead of you, so remember what I said. If this baby is a boy, you run. Go to Pons Aelius and knock on the door of the orphanage. Tell them your family died and they will take you in."

I began to shake. I was so scared. Was being married so terrible? "What about Anna?"

Mother smoothed down my hair. "She will be fine, darling. She is much older than you and at an age to marry. But you must not."

I felt a tingle and watched as Mother set a necklace around my neck. It was warm and heavy-- A golden owl on a leather cord. When I looked back up at my mother, her face contorted to pain again and her grip became overly tight, making me squirm and attempt to get away from her as she doubled over.

She reached up and tucked the necklace beneath the collar of my dress and a few moments later when her look of pain subsided, she turned and left slowly, sliding the stable door closed behind her.

I untucked the necklace she had given me and inspected it. It wasn't just warm from sitting at my chest; it seemed to give off a heat of its own, warming my fingers as I ran them over the ridges that defined the owl. I had never seen anything so beautiful.

A sound beyond the stable door, had me tucking it back under my collar before the door slid open and a large man stepped inside.

He wore thick padded clothes and had a sword at his hip. He grinned when he saw me. "Hello there, little one. Is your name Morgana?"

"Yes, sir," I said.

"So polite. Tell me, would you like to go for a ride?"

A chill ran down my spine. The man was staring at me in a way that I didn't like. My stepfather would be angry if I was rude to his guest, but I knew I couldn't go anywhere with this man. Something inside me told me so.

"Thank you, sir, let me just check with my stepfather."

I ran past him and out of the stable before he could say another word. I was small but lithe and that always served me well.

My legs carried me back to the castle and up to my room where I shut the door and grabbed a few of my things. Between my mother's words and the way the man leered at me, a panic had settled in my bones.

I heard a scream echo through the castle. It was my mother's. I dropped the satchel and ran, following her screams through the stone hallways. A few servants passed me, going about their business as if nothing was amiss. I ran until I stopped in front of a closed door. Mother was definitely beyond the door, but I paused unsure if I wanted to open it.

I bit my lip and took a deep breath, my shaking hand rising to the latch. I flicked it up and pressed the door open a few inches.

Inside I saw a large woman standing at the foot of the bed and my mother, sweaty and red-faced, lying on the bed, propped up on pillows. She had stopped screaming, and the room was dead silent for a long moment. The air in the room seemed charged like the calm right before the first crash of thunder in a storm. A tiny cry rang out, breaking the silence, and the large woman moved from the end of the bed to the side, carrying a small bundle. A baby swaddled in a blanket.

"It's a boy, ma'am. Lord Pendragon will be pleased." She set the baby down in my mother's arms. "I'll inform him right away."

The large woman turned towards the door and I stepped back, pressing myself against the wall until she walked out and continued down the hall. I pushed the door open and tiptoed inside. My mother was staring fondly down and the baby in her arms. Her hair was wet with sweat, but she was beautiful, none-the-less.

"Mother," I whispered, and her head tipped up to catch my eye. The smile drained from her face.

"Oh, sweet girl. Run. Run now and never look back. Please!"

My heart raced at her words. "But mother..."

"No, Morgana, there is no time. You must go now. Run straight into the woods and don't stop. RUN!"

Her voice set fire to my legs. I turned and bolted. My feet slapping on the stones as I careened through the halls toward my room. I planned to grab my things and go, but a strong pair of arms circled me, lifting my feet from the ground.

"Where are you going, little one?"

CHAPTER TWO

The hot stench of his breath burned my nose, and I writhed trying to escape his grasp. "Stop that," he said, his voice suddenly cold.

The command stopped my fighting, but my heart still raced, ready to run as soon as I could.

"That's better," he said, setting my feet on the ground, but his hand wrapped fully around my upper arm and lifted painfully so I couldn't run.

The tall man squatted down in front of me. "A lady never runs. You should know better than that at your age. Where are you going?"

"I'm sorry, sir. My father asked me to get a letter from his office." I lied. I didn't know why the lie came so easily, but I prayed it was convincing.

The man studied my face for a moment and then tucked a strand of my red hair behind my ear. "All right,

Morgana. But be sure to always walk from now on. You aren't a child anymore and no one should ever see you as such."

Another chill went down my spine. "Of course, sir. I'm sorry."

The man smiled, then rose to his feet and released me. I dropped my head and turned, walking down the hall, though I could feel his eyes on my back like daggers. I continued in the direction of my father's office until I moved around a corner that would cut me from his sight. Then I stopped and pressed against the wall, waiting to make sure he had left. I peeked back around the corner and saw him disappear around another corner.

I dashed back and into my room, grabbing my things, then after ensuring the hallway was clear, raced to the stairs, down and out through the kitchen. Then I ran straight across the castle courtyard and out into the forest.

The air was muggy and hot, but I didn't stop. I forced my legs forward as I dodged trees and hopped fallen logs. The birds sang from the treetops and grouse fluttered away as I scared them from their hiding places.

My lungs burned like fire and my muscles screamed at me to stop, but I knew, somehow, deep down, that if I stopped running bad things would happen to me. The pain in my legs was nothing compared to what I would suffer at the hands of that man. So, I continued to run, heading toward the ocean. The city lay on its shores and I knew the orphanage was there, near the church with the tall steeple. Mother had told me once that if I was ever in trouble, I could go there, and they would take care of me. It was as if she had known someday, I would be in trouble. It was a safe place for children.

By the afternoon, I could only walk and even that was getting difficult. I needed somewhere to hide so I could rest without being found.

My eyes scanned the rocky areas, looking for a small crevice or crack I could slip into, somewhere small enough that if anyone trying to find me would dismiss it. I had once hidden from my sister that way, sliding between the wall of the stable and a stack of hay. She hadn't found me for hours; I had fallen asleep when my angry father finally found me. He had swept me up in his arms and told me how foolish it was to hide so well when I wasn't in trouble.

Now that I was in trouble, I needed to do that again. I climbed a rocky outcropping, skinning my knee and tearing the hem of my dress, but finally found a small rocky space just wide enough that I could fit in sideways if I pressed hard. Beyond the opening, it was only wide enough that I could sit down, but it was cool in the shaded place and my heart rate began to slow at the feeling of safety it offered.

I used the bottom hem of my dress to wipe the blood from my knee. It wasn't a deep wound and would be fine, though it stung.

The satchel I had brought with me only had a sweater and a small knife I stole from the kitchen a month ago and tucked under my bed. I had no idea at the time why I had stolen it. It seemed absurd, but something demanded I have it and now I was glad. The knife would be useful if I needed to live in the forest for long. The coast was a long way off on foot; at least a three-day walk, less if I could run most of the way.

I pulled off my boots awkwardly in the tight space but getting my feet free felt good. I rubbed my sore toes and then tucked my boots in beside me. It was warm enough to leave them off, even in the dark crack of the rock.

My knees came up tight to my chest, and I dropped my head onto them, closing my eyes and letting out a deep breath. The shaking in my legs from overexertion finally calmed, and I drifted off.

When I woke, the sun had set and there was a chill in the air. I turned to face the crack I had slipped through and stretched out my legs. They were stiff and seized from the cramped position I had fallen asleep in.

I leaned back and noticed the warm weight of the necklace my mother had given me. My fingers retrieved it from beneath my collar and traced the ridges. I could remember my mother wearing it always. Even as a very small child, I saw it sparkling at her throat. My smaller hands would always reach for it like it was a star in the sky.

The sound of horses' hooves snapped me out of my memory, and I held my breath, listening.

"Morgana?" It was my stepfather's voice. "Where are you, child?"

I stayed silent and still.

More voices called out farther away, calling my name. My heart began to race. I felt trapped in the tiny cave. Many men out searching for me. If one of them found me, they would take me back to the castle. Bile rose in my throat. Uther would marry me to that vile man.

A flash of myself, older but dirty and locked away in a dark place popped into my mind. My face was dirty and tear-streaked. Steel bars kept me a prisoner. A shudder shook my body, and I pushed the image away. Mother always said I had a vivid imagination, but that felt different. It felt real.

I pulled my knees back up carefully, making sure no part of me was visible outside of the crevice. Even though it was dark outside, I couldn't risk someone seeing the colour of my dress or the shape of my foot.

I stayed frozen like that for a long time, praying none of the men would find me.

Eventually the sound of horses and men calling faded and disappeared. They were going the way I wanted to go, leaving me stuck in my hiding place. I had no food or water, but I would stay put until it was safe.

I let my head rest on the hard rock and fell asleep again.

The next time my eyes opened, the sun was up. I sat for a long time, listening for men or horses. The birds sang merrily in the trees outside my cave, but no other sounds.

I crept out, stumbling on my numb legs, a chill in my bones until I made it to a ray of sun that shone through the trees and splashed on a flat rock. There, I sat down and let the morning light warm me while the feeling returned to my legs.

Loneliness sunk deep. I could never go back to Lord Pendragon's castle -- to my mother or my baby sister. I could track down Anna and see if her new husband would let me live with them, but I had no idea where she had gone. My best bet was to go to the orphanage, as mother had said.

I pulled on my boots, rose and began walking towards the sea. The day was pleasant, though warm, and most of the day I walked through the forest. My short legs were easily tired, but I forced them on. It would be at least two more days before I got there if I kept this pace and I had no food or water.

I had the small knife from the kitchen, but that was no help to me since I couldn't catch anything in the forest. If I found a river, I could catch a fish. Long days swimming with my sisters had taught me that skill, though I hadn't fished in the year since my father died and mother remarried. I was sure I could catch one. So, I continued walking until my legs threatened to give out, then walked further still.

I was so desperate by midafternoon, that I climbed a very large tree, the tallest I could find. When I reached the top, it swayed and danced in the wind, but I held on tight and looked around.

From my place high in the tree, I felt like the queen of the world. The whole valley lay out before me, a blanket of green on rolling hills divided by rocky outcroppings.

A river ran to the south, I could see. It was not too far, so I climbed back down, tearing my dress again in my haste, and began walking that way.

It was still an hour before I reached the river, but at the shore, I dropped to my knees and drank deep of the fresh cool waters. I drank until my stomach ached and then splashed water on my burnt face. Even beneath the forest canopy, the sun had burned my cheeks and my nose. It was the struggle of being fair-skinned and red-haired, my mother always said.

Once I felt refreshed, I turned and headed east again. I broke into a light jog as the sun would set in a few hours and I needed to be much further along than I was. At least I assumed so, having no clue where I actually was.

I kept my jog light, dodging low branches and thistles as the forest gave way into a long flat plain. The sun setting at my back assured me I was heading in the right direction, but I didn't recall a flat area like the one I was in when we travelled this way after my father's death. I was hesitant to cross as I would have nowhere to hide if one of my stepfather's riders was still out looking for me, but the way around would take me either far north or far south, adding days to my travel.

I sat down on a fallen tree and considered my options. My stomach growled and churned, reminding me I hadn't eaten in far too long. I fiddled with my mother's necklace, tracing the swoop of the owl's wing, over and over beneath my thumb.

"What should I do?" I asked no one in particular.

An image of me racing across the open field filled my mind. The vision didn't show anyone chasing me or any other trouble, so I accepted that as my choice. Unsure if it was intuition or my mother sending me instructions from afar, I decided not to second guess it.

I rose to my feet and dashed forward.

CHAPTER THREE

Present

"Where is my mother's necklace, now?" I asked Merlin. He was astride his grey horse and I on Copper as we moved through the snowy terrain.

He reached into his pocket and presented the necklace from my memory. It glittered in the sun and spun on the end of its leather lash. I pressed Copper forward and reached out, taking the necklace from his hand. It was cold for a moment and then heated suddenly, surprising me.

Copper snorted and tossed his head.

"Easy, boy." He settled but his pace increased, passing Merlin and leading the way. "What's the matter with you?"

Merlin chuckled. "Your horse is made fully of magic now. Two kinds of magic. He can sense the magic in the necklace, and it's given him a new lease on life... if you will."

"What does that mean?" I asked, stroking Copper's neck.

"It means, your horse is not alive in a conventional way. He lives on magic and that necklace is pure magic."

I ran my thumb over the golden owl. "He is alive! How can he not be?"

Merlin was silent for a long time. So long that I finally worked up the nerve and looked at him. He was studying me. "There is more to magic than you know. More than you should ever know. But you will learn, there is no stopping it now. Your horse is not alive."

A stab of pain and guilt hit my chest. My horse was here, but not alive. He was still dead, killed by a horrible man in a horrible way. That brought fresh tears for the old wound.

"Don't cry, Morgana. I'm sure he would rather be with you, anyway."

Rather than resting peacefully in the ever after? I wasn't convinced, but the selfish part of me was glad to have him. I didn't want to continue this journey on some other horse.

My fingers tangled in his mane for a moment before I gave in and let myself drop onto his neck. He felt the same as he did before--warm and soft. His coat was thick for winter, but I pressed the necklace against his neck and his gait became animated as it did when I was using powerful dark arts magic. I couldn't keep my sorrow when he arched his neck and began to prance through the snow. A laugh bubbled up and out, breaking the icy silence of the open plains around us.

Merlin's horse had to trot to keep up with us and Copper huffed, increasing his pace so as not to let the grey mare pass him. Before long we were racing across the snow, my laughter hysterical. When I looked back, Merlin was grinning, too, his eyes dancing with the humour.

We raced for several minutes before Merlin brought his horse back to a trot.

"Whoa," I said to Copper who obeyed right away, slowing until he was walking again. He was breathing heavily, but luckily we hadn't run enough to make him sweat. The Sun was warming, but the day was still too cold for him to have sweat without catching a chill.

I caught myself on that thought. If he was made of magic, would he catch a chill? Could he go all day and never tire?

"What are you thinking?" Merlin's voice pulled me from my thoughts.

"Nothing," I said.

"Oh no, I know you better than that, Morgana."

It was strange to only have fragments of memory of him when he had knowledge of me. "I don't like that you know me so well and I've just met you," I said with a scowl.

"Then back you go, pick up where you left off and organize your memories properly. We have a long way to travel, you might as well get all the way through it."

I wanted to ask him where we were going, but remembering my past was a bigger draw, I let my mind slipped back to the open field I was running through at dusk on my way to the coast.

CHAPTER FOUR

Ten years earlier.

It was full dark by the time I reached the far side of the flatlands and had been dark for a while. I was lucky I hadn't stepped in any holes and twisted my ankle, but my legs were shaking as I collapsed to the ground.

I lay in the cool grass breathing deeply and decided that was a fine place to rest for the night, curled up beneath a tall pine. The moon shone through the branches, making sharp patterns as I stared up at it. My stomach had stopped screaming for food, which I was thankful for, but I felt so weak and tired.

I was nodding off when I heard a rustle and twig snap. Despite the pain in my legs, I shot up, ready to run away, but a voice stopped me.

"I've just come to help you." It was a man, his face obscured by the forest and darkness.

"Who are you?" I asked, backing until I bumped into a poplar tree.

"My name is Merlin. We will meet later, but I just wanted to leave this for you." He set down something wrapped in cloth, then turned and strode away.

I stood against the poplar tree, my heart racing in my chest until long after I could no longer hear his footsteps; until the night sounds of the forest seemed to be overly loud.

I took one step forward towards the wrapped package he had left, then another. Crouching down, I poked it as if it might be a snake and would bite me. When nothing happened, I unwrapped the cloth and discovering it contained a loaf of bread and a flask of water.

I grabbed the items and turned, racing through the forest until I was farther away from the place the man had been. I had no idea why he would have left the food and water for me or how he knew I needed them, but I would worry about that later--once I was safe.

When my legs would no longer carry me, I stumbled to the ground and brought the bread to my mouth. It was fresh and soft, with a light crust on the outside. It must have been freshly baked and my stomach almost revolted at the sudden influx of food, but I washed it down with the cool water in the flask and willed my body to accept it. I ate half the loaf sitting there on the forest's dirt floor, thankful for the kindness of a stranger.

His words floated back to me, he said we would meet later. Did that mean he was following me? I was confused but stopped chewing and listened carefully in case he was following even now. I heard nothing. Not a step or a snap or a shuffle.

I wrapped up the rest of the loaf of bread and capped the water flask to save some for the morning, though there wasn't much left. If I found a stream the next day, I could refill it.

I curled up where I lay and tried to concentrate on the sounds of the forest to listen for anyone tracking me, but my body was weary and my mind worse, so eventually I slipped into sleep despite my efforts.

When I awoke, the sun was filtering through the trees. I rose and stretched, feeling the tension in my muscles, then strode on towards the east, determined to make as much progress as possible that day. While I walked, I nibbled the bread and sipped the water sparingly. I had to make it last. The bread might be all I would eat that day, and the water needed to last until I found a stream.

My mind wandered as the birds sang in the treetops. I tried to fill in the gaps in the man's face, which I couldn't see the night before. His words rang through my mind. Who was he?

Eventually, I came to the road that I knew led to the coast and the city of Pons Aelius. The road was well-travelled and crossed clear to the other side of the country, so I let myself daydream as I walked the long road. I imagined my life once I was grown. I knew mother would come for me when she could and bring Elaine and maybe our new brother if he survived. We could be a family again.

My boot caught on a root and I tripped, falling to my knees before rising and dusting off my skirt. Both my knees were torn now, and the hem of my skirt was ripped nearly off. It trailed behind me on the ground as I walked. Hopefully, the orphanage would have some clothes for me.

I stopped at a river and refilled the flask around midday, then continued walking. By nightfall, the sun had burnt me to a crisp again and my legs wobbled beneath me, but as I came over a rise, I stared down at the city of

Pons Aelius. The sea crashing waves against the shore on the far side.

"I did it," I whispered taking a few more steps before the world got fuzzy and I collapsed, falling into darkness.

"Wake up, little sorceress," a man's voice whispered.

My eyelids were too heavy and refused to lift.

"You've made it now. I suppose you might as well rest. I'll see you in a few months once you have settled into your new life here and I am finished with my work. Until then, keep your necklace hidden and do not, under any circumstance, use magic."

I wanted to reply or ask him what he meant about me using magic, but I was too tired and instead fell asleep.

When I woke again, it surprised me to find I was in a small room with many beds. Each pallet bed had a coloured blanket, and all were in neat rows and tidy. I rose to my feet, and the room spun for a moment before everything settled and I crossed the room to the door.

I took the hall to a set of stairs that went straight down. At the bottom, I heard people talking and followed the voices.

"You know, the children should be thankful for what they have instead of complaining about what they don't have," an older woman said.

"Mmm-hmm. You are absolutely right. This will teach them to be grateful," a second, younger-sounding woman replied.

I tiptoed to the door and peeked around the corner. The women were facing away from the doorway, sipping teas and rocking in rocking chairs. I peered past them and could see out the window, children beating rugs and scrubbing the flagstone steps.

I took a few more steps forward and cleared my throat to announce my presence.

The younger woman turned to look at me. "Oh, good, you're up."

The older woman glared at me, though, with an evil expression. "This one doesn't have to work?" she sneered.

"She just came in last night. A very handsome man found her on the road and delivered her here. I tried to convince him to stay for a while, but he said he was in a hurry."

"Hmm, well she looks fine now. If I were you, I would get her started before she thinks she will just sit around here and do nothing."

The younger woman glanced back at me before nodding to the older woman. "You can go help the rest of the children clean, you know how to clean, don't you?"

I bowed my head. "Yes ma'am, but I've worked in the stables for the last year."

"Excellent," she chirped clapping her hands. "You can go see the army livery commander and see if he can have a use for you. If you can be useful, he will give you a few shillings a week and that can be your contribution to the household."

I bowed my head again. "Which way are the stables, Ma'am?"

"Out the door and head towards the ocean, you will see it."

The older woman grinned as though the younger woman had done something brilliant and it pleased her.

I didn't know that people could get paid for working in the stables. Perhaps that would be my future. I loved being around horses.

I stepped out of the house and glanced back at the tall building. It was as high as the castle, but it was made of wood instead of stone. Its plaster was faded and crumbling, but it would be my home. My safe place. I passed the rest of the children who continued to work, but I felt their eyes track me.

"Where are you going?" a tall boy asked, stepping in front of me.

"To the livery," I replied, stepping to the side to go around him.

"Humph, we'll see how long you last there. Probably get trampled before the day is done." The group of older boys around him all laughed too, but I wasn't worried. I had spent the last year tending horses. Surely it wouldn't be much different.

I walked through the city, amazed by the people in fine clothes and polished horses pulling elegant carriages. There were also plenty of soldiers on horseback. The closer I got to the water, the more soldiers I found until I came to a large fenced area. The fence was made of logs stood on end to encircle the area. Horses hooves pounded, ringing from the other side and I moved along the fence until I found my way into the livery courtyard and right up to the stable doors.

I unlatched the door and pulled it open. Men in uniforms were hurrying about, grooming horses and polishing irons.

"Excuse me," I said to a burly man with a long thick beard.

He looked up from his work and narrowed his eyes on me. "What are you doing here, girl?" His two front teeth were missing.

I took a step back and bumped into another man who continued walking with a horse's bridle over his shoulder as if I weren't there.

"I'm here to find work. I've been working in--"

My words cut off at the man's loud laughter. "You've come to find work? What are you? 40 pounds? How the hell will you do anything here?"

I opened my mouth to speak again, but he cut me off once more.

"Go on, get out of here. If you have an older brother, send him along instead."

I paused for a moment, but he growled like a mad dog and I turned on my heel, running back toward the door.

"Loose horse!" someone yelled behind me. I spun and came face to face with a giant bay horse barrelling towards me. My mind told my legs to move out of the way, but fear froze me in place, unable to move at all as the horse got closer and closer. His hooves, as large as my head, pounded the earth with exaggerated movements.

Finally, something clicked, and I raised my arms and yelled "Whoa!"

The horse skidded to a stop in front of me, dust billowing up from the ground to sting at my eyes and up my nose. I reached up with a shaking hand and grabbed the reins, the horse thankfully keeping his head low. He could have easily lifted me off the ground with his massive head or stepped on me to get past.

"Did you see that?" someone said.

"That kid just stopped the commander's horse."

"What the hell is a girl doing in here?" Many voices spoke over each other, but they seemed distant.

"Who are you?" A burly man with a bright red hat bent at the waist to look me in the eye. I was still shaking and shocked by the horse running at me.

The man took the horse's reins from me and rested his large meaty hand on my shoulder. My eyes dropped from his hat to his face.

He grinned. "What's your name, girl?"

I licked my lips and cleared my throat before whispering, "Morgana."

"What are you doing here?" he asked.

The horse stomped his foot and blew warm wet air from his nose.

"I came to get a job tending horses, sir." My voice was still shaky, but louder now.

The big man huffed, and I expected him to turn me away, so it was a complete shock when he turned to the rest of the men who had gathered in the stable aisle to watch and said, "Morgana here is our new stable boy...err...girl. You all look out for her and don't give her any trouble."

His voice was harsh and booming like my stepfather's, but his words were some I had never heard from Uther. This big army commander was not only giving me a job but sticking up for me.

A round of "yes, sirs" echoed through the stable, and the big man turned back to me.

"My name is Commander Artorius. And this," he said stroking the horse's neck as it stomped the ground, "is Fargo. He's a mean old horse, but he is important to me. You be sure and take care of him first, you hear me?"

"Yes, sir, commander, sir," I stuttered.

"Good, I'll see you first thing tomorrow morning. Be here before the sun comes up and don't be late." He straightened to his full height, staring down at me. He was a mountain of a man; his sword probably weighed more than I did.

"Yes, sir." I turned and forced myself to walk, not run, from the stable. Looking back at the last moment to catch one more glimpse of the big bay stallion that had nearly ended my life.

CHAPTER FIVE

I ran back to the orphanage, pleased with myself for getting the job, but also worried that the horses were much wilder than what I was used to.

I passed all the other children in the yard, still scrubbing and cleaning the front of the orphanage. The tall boy who had spoken to me before was missing and I was thankful. His smirking face was unpleasant.

I walked through the door and down the hall to the sitting room the women had been drinking tea in. Now only the younger woman was sitting in there. She rocked and hummed as she sewed up some clothing.

"Excuse me, Ma'am," I said, startling her.

"Oh, yes, hello, dear. Were you able to get a job at the stables?"

"Yes, ma'am. I start in the morning."

"Oh, thank goodness. That old bat would never let it go if one of you didn't have some kind of paying work." She shook her head. "What is your name, anyway?"

"Morgana, ma'am."

"Very well, you can call me Lady Ethel. I run this home for abandoned children. You are expected to clean up after yourself and help with chores, but your main duty will be at the stables. I better not hear anything about you slacking off there." She didn't sound very stern, but I had learned that some people could act one way sometimes and a completely different way at other times, so I was polite.

"Yes, Ma'am."

"Alright, now go to the kitchen and have some breakfast. The girls have been cooking."

I thanked her and turned, following the voices until I found the kitchen. The room was as large as the dining hall in my stepfather's castle. Nearly two dozen children were moving about. The youngest were all seated at one of two tables, and the older ones were cooking over an open fireplace. I had helped my mother cook enough times when I was small that I could cook decently, but it looked like they had it all in hand, so instead, I began filling mugs with water and setting them on the table at each chair. By the time I was done, the food was ready.

I sat down between a small girl of no more than 4 and a girl my age who had copper coloured hair and delicate features. She was busy talking with a painfully slim boy. His face was gaunt, and he seemed quiet and soft-spoken. I assumed that was why he was sitting at this table instead of the one with the rowdy boys. I didn't blame him. The biggest and loudest boy at the other table shoved another boy out of a chair so he could sit at the head of the table.

"That's Eli. Stay out of his way," the girl beside me whispered.

I turned to look at her, but she was already back to her conversation with the slim boy.

Eggs and bread with milk was a standard breakfast, and I was glad to see that the orphanage fed us things I was used to and enjoyed.

We all ate quickly; the sound of spoons on plates rang through the room until we had eaten our food, then the volume rose as the children stacked dishes beside the water pail for washing and the rowdy boys, including Eli, ran off to do whatever chores they had after breakfast. I stayed in the kitchen, with two other girls including the one who I had sat beside.

The younger children wandered off towards the sitting room, I assumed to play or listen to stories or whatever young children did in an orphanage.

"What's your name?" the pretty girl with copper hair asked.

"Morgana," I replied.

"My name is Lily, and this is Breena." She pointed to the black-haired girl whose back was to me. Breena was already scrubbing dishes in the barrel.

"Good to meet you," she said, never turning around.

"It's good to meet you two, too," I said. "How long have you lived here?"

Lily rolled up her sleeves and stepped in beside Breena, so I did the same, standing on the other side of Breena and picking up a cloth to dry the bowls and cups.

"I've been here for two years," Lily said. "Lady Ethel is the nicest lady I have ever met, but you'd be wise to stay away from Mistress Carlyle. She will tan your hide for glancing at her."

I bit my lip and tucked that information away and would be sure never to look at Mistress Carlyle. I imagined she was the older woman that Lady Ethel had been speaking to in the parlour when I woke.

We continued our work until all the dishes were clean and put away; then the girls began chopping meat and vegetables, so I helped where I could.

The orphanage didn't have a midday meal, so we worked around the house, cleaning and scrubbing the rest of the day. By evening my stomach was growling.

The boys all came racing through the door, skidding to a stop as they reached the table. Then they jeered and jostled each other. The thin boy came in last. His soft eyes a stark contrast to the rest of them.

He sat down beside a toddler and grinned at him, holding his little fingers.

I sat beside the thin boy, drawn to his soft nature.

"What's your name?" I asked.

"Leruis," he replied in a hushed voice before turning his attention back to the child.

Lady Ethel swept into the room, her long skirt whispering across the floor. She was as elegant as my mother, but younger and had a lightness to her I hadn't seen in my mother since my father died. The children were all hushed as she seated herself. A toddler slipped out of his chair across from me and waddled over to Lady Ethel. His grubby hand patted her hip, and she scooped him up to sit on her lap.

We all ate quietly after that. There was something about Lady Ethel that captivated me. She didn't raise her voice or demand anything of us, but all the children, myself included, felt her presence and softness. I studied her as she fed the toddler in her arms, his little mouth opening wide to take in the spoonful of stew as if he was a baby bird in a nest.

My muscles relaxed at the peace I felt. I missed my mother and sisters, but Lady Ethel took away the sting. When we finished dinner, Lady Ethel sent us to bed. I was dirtier than the rest of the children and wished I could bathe before I climbed into the pallet, but with everyone hurrying to their beds, I was swept up in the rush.

Lady Ethel came in, carrying a book. She sat down in an old rocking chair as all the children settled in their beds.

I lay on my side and watched her, praying she would read aloud as my father used to do and, as soon as silence fell, that was exactly what she did.

She read us a story of dragons and pirates and heroes. I fell asleep before the end, but I will never forget the magical tales she told us, nor the whisper of magic that seemed to hang over me as I drifted off to sleep.

The next morning, I rose with the rest of the children but dashed out of the house without breakfast. I would be late if I waited around and I couldn't be late on my first day with a real job.

My boots slapped on the packed earth as I careened through the city towards the ocean. The log walls on the army stables came into view and I slowed to a jog. The sun was peeking over the horizon but hadn't fully risen, so I wasn't late.

I pulled open the stable door and the warm scent of horses filled my nose. My shoulders dropped and my muscles relaxed as the dozens of horses nickered lowly.

I found a pitchfork and climbed a ladder to the haymow and began throwing down hay with enthusiasm. The horses kept nickering. I climbed down and used the fork to shove hay into the stalls closest to the chute, then climbed back up when I realized I would need much more hay.

Voices echoed from down below and I paused in my work to let them pass beneath the chute.

A man's face looked up at me. It was the burly man with the long beard who I had met the night before.

I waved awkwardly, and he grinned, displaying his missing front teeth.

"You come down here now, girl, and I'll shove that hay down. You can give it to the horses," he said.

"All right," I took my pitchfork and climbed down the ladder. When I was about five feet from the ground, the man's hands came around my waist and he pried me off the ladder. I squeaked, but he set me on the ground and gave my hair a ruffle. Then he grabbed another pitchfork and climbed the ladder with much more grace than I expected from the large man.

"By the way," he called down from the loft. "My name is Jag."

"Okay." I began the task of forking hay into each stall; it was much faster with Jag shoving large amounts of hay from the loft.

"You have enough there now?" he called down.

"Yes, sir," I replied.

A few other men were in the stalls now, grooming horses, and they chuckled at my words.

"What?" I asked.

They all went back to their work, grooming the horses to a brilliant shine, so, I returned to my work as well. Once every horse had enough hay for the day, I went about gathering water from the cement cistern outside the stable. It was a much faster way to water the horses, so I was done with that chore by noon.

By then the stable was full of men in uniform, including one man in a broad-brimmed hat who all the men called sir. He seemed in charge of the training of the horses, directing soldiers to take their horses out to the log corral where I discovered they did all their training and riding.

I set to work cleaning stalls while the horses were out. They had a wheeled cart that I could push down the aisle from stall to stall. It was designed for a man, so I struggled to dump it, but once I figured out how much was a reasonable size load, the task was manageable.

I was just washing my hands in a bucket and wondering if I could go back to the orphanage to get something to eat when Lady Ethel arrived.

"Morgana, I brought you lunch, dear."

I dried my hands on my dirty skirt and raced toward her. She had attracted the attention of several of the soldiers who had been standing around the riding area watching the men train the horses.

"Let me through," I demanded as they blocked my path. No one seemed to notice me, so I moved along the circle of burly men until I found Jag. I yanked on his arm and he glanced down at me.

"What is it?" he asked.

"She has MY lunch," I complained, drawing attention away from lady Ethel.

"Morgana!" she scolded. "That is no way for a young lady to speak."

Jag laughed and lifted me onto his broad shoulder. "Don't worry, ma'am. She has to be more forceful if she's going to hang with this lot, don't you, little girl?" The rest of the men laughed, but I just clung to Jag's head. I was up much too high, and he was barely holding me.

"Oh, you silly man. Put that girl down so she can eat her lunch. Leave the rough-housing to boys."

Jag laughed again and set me down in front of him. Lady Ethel handed me something wrapped in cloth and I pushed past Jag to go eat it. The men were towering over me and it was uncomfortable. "Thank you, Lady Ethel," I called over my shoulder, remembering my manners at the last moment.

She hardly noticed though as the big men had gone back to talking to her. I crossed to the corral gate. Beyond I could hear men yelling and the sound of hooves pounding. I climbed the wooden slats, tucking my lunch under my arm and intending to eat perched on the top of the gate.

Once I scrambled up and got turned around to sit on the top rail, I glanced out across the area and nearly fell right back off the gate.

The men had the horses hog-tied. Some of them were struggling. Others had broken free, and the men were chasing them down. Their flanks were all soaked with foamy sweat and the man in the broad-brimmed hat, whom all these tough men had been calling sir, was standing in the middle of the chaos whipping a horse who lay on his side refusing to rise.

CHAPTER SIX

Present.

"I don't want to remember anymore." I lay forward, draping myself over Copper's neck. The fear in the horses' eyes had been too much. It reminded me of how I imagined Copper's final moments and fresh tears sprung to my eyes.

Merlin chuckled. "What part are you at?"

I sat up and looked at him and he frowned. "What is it?"

I sighed. "The men were harsh. I knew they had been harsh, I remembered that, but not the exact extent of it. How is it possible that some of my memory was erased, but parts remain? I had forgotten about Lady Ethel, too. My only memory from the orphanage had been of Mistress Carlyle."

"You will get to that. It's better if you remember in sequence. Then nothing will be left out."

"But how did I lose all these memories in the first place? Did you do magic on me?"

Merlin studied me for a moment. "No, Morgana. I did not do any magic on you."

I made an exasperated noise. "This is frustrating. Can't you just give me the highlights?"

"Nope, sorry. We should find a place to stop for the night, though. I think there is a city not too far."

"I'm not sure a city is a good idea," I said, remembering what I did to the Roman soldiers on Avalon.

Merlin grinned and his eyes twinkled. "Don't worry about it. I'll just change your appearance a bit."

I bit my lip. "A bit how?"

"Magic, of course."

"Yes. I figured it was magic, but how will you change it?" I asked.

"You'll see."

He began to whistle a jolly tune, and I sighed. I spent some time thinking about how I had brought Copper back to life. I'd used a magic word that had repaired my burnt and torn papers back on Avalon. But that seemed quite different from bringing back a whole horse. Copper seemed the same, mostly. His eyes were different, but he listened to all my cues and felt the same otherwise. I scratched his withers, and he stretched his neck out as he always did, his top lip quivering with the pleasure of having his itchy places scratched. I giggled and continued scratching him until my fingers were dark with dander and dirt. He would need good, thorough grooming soon.

I pondered the idea that he wasn't alive but still produced dander and heat. It was strange, but, in the end, I decided not to dwell on it. I had found him again and felt like the world was right.

"There," Merlin said as we breached a hill.

"The snow is deep at the bottom," I said, watching the wind whip through the gully between us and the city.

"We will make it. Just hang on tight to that magic horse of yours. Sara has never failed me."

Merlin's mare snorted and jogged forward as though she was ready to attack the snowdrifts. Her coat was nearly as white as the snow, but I noticed she had a patch of dark flecks that began at the tip of her right ear and moved down her neck to her shoulder. I had never seen a horse marked that way.

"What kind of marking is that, on your horse?" I asked.

Merlin grinned and stroked his hand down the horse's arched neck. "It's called a bloody shoulder mark. I will tell you a story."

Something about those words sounded familiar as if he had told me many stories before.

"A powerful Sheik of a war-like tribe went riding along in the desert on his favourite horse, a milk-white mare of breathtaking beauty. To be the favourite of such a man, she was wonderful indeed and apart from her beauty, must have proven herself in battle as a worthy mount for her warrior master."

"The Sheik and his mare travelled far into the desert and there, by bad luck, encountered a small party led by a rival chieftain. A battle to the death was inevitable and the scorched silence was broken by the clashing of two razor-sharp blades as the fierce opponents wheeled their horses and struck. On and on the battle raged, for they were evenly matched, fearless fighters and superb horsemen both. Each blade found several marks, and each man was wounded. Finally, the Sheik on the milk-white mare drove through his opponent's guard and his sword struck his adversary's throat.

"Silently, his followers wrapped their master's body in his cloak, draped it across his stallion's ornate saddle and rode away, leaving the victor swaying on the white mare, bleeding from two terrible wounds. His left chest and shoulder were sliced to the bone and there was another cruel gash on the right side of his back, just above the waist. From both wounds welled dark red blood, which flowed down the mare's silky shoulder and flank and dripped on to the sand.

"The Sheik felt darkness rushing in and he reeled in the saddle. The little mare began to walk home, slowly and carefully. For a day and a night, she continued, picking her way delicately so as not to disturb the precarious balance of her beloved master who slumped in the saddle, his life's blood oozing down and away, soaking into the desert sand.

"The mare brought him back to camp, but his wounds had been mortal and when his followers lifted him down, he was dead.

"That night, in the quiet desert a little way from the grieving camp, the mare foaled and next morning, the tribe were awestruck to find she has given birth to a colt with chestnut markings that exactly matched the way his dam's shoulder had been stained by her dying master's blood.

"Legend has it that the dead Sheik arranged with the Gods that his mare's dedication would be commended so that forever after, any descendant of hers who was possessed of outstanding courage or ability would bear the bloodstains as a mark of honour."

I stared at the beautiful mare. She was exotic looking with her dark mane and tail and snow-white coat. Her forelock was long and swept across her face in stark contrast.

The horses reached the bottom of the hill; the snow blowing across the path bit into my skin and I tucked my face against my tiger skin. Merlin's horse was ahead of Copper and the little grey mare trudged hard through the snowdrifts, jumping with each step. She forged a path that was much easier for Copper to travel. I gripped his mane as he jumped in the same places the mare had, following her tracks exactly.

The sun was low and blinding ahead, but we continued until some low trees slowed the wind, making it howl in an eerie cry. Finally, past the worst of it, the snow levelled out. Copper and Sara were puffing, their sides heaving, but the grey mare had a fierce look in her eye, as though she would slay a dragon if she saw one.

The city ahead was busy with people and horses, but Merlin stopped just outside the city and Copper stopped next to Sara, reaching over and sniffing her nose. She pinned her ears and screamed at him in a sharp display of her disinterest. I laughed but when I caught Merlin's eyes; he was staring at me, his face serious and his lips whispering words I couldn't hear.

His hand reached out, his mouth still moving, and his finger touched my forehead as he had when he brought back my memories. A tingle swept through me from my forehead down to my toes.

He dropped his hand and grinned with a sparkle in his eye.

"What did you do?" I asked looking down at myself.

"You'll see," he said as he led the way into the city.

I wanted to demand he tell me, but Sara was jogging away, so I pressed Copper and he happily jogged to catch up, his ears pricked forward and eyes locked on the grey mare's hindquarters. I shook my head but couldn't help giggle at my silly horse. He had a horse crush on the pretty mare.

Copper and I followed Merlin through the city until he stopped at an Inn. He swung off his mare and handed her off to a boy at the stable door.

I slid from Copper's back and had an awful sense of repeating old mistakes when another boy came out to collect Copper. Of course, my horse wasn't wearing a halter or bridle, so the boy had to scurry back into the stable and get a rope.

"He'll be fine, Morgana," Merlin said, standing close to me.

I bit my lip, unsure how he had known anything about what had happened, but that was a question for later. My fingers pulled my mother's necklace off and tied it securely in his mane. I wasn't sure what made me do it, but as soon as it was done, I felt like he was protected. As if my mother was watching over him. I stroked his neck as the young boy put the rope over his neck and led him inside.

Merlin took my freezing cold hand in his and led me to the door of the inn before dropping my hand and opening the door.

Inside the air was hot and humid. A fire raged in the fireplace, and men and women sat around at small tables in the long and narrow room.

Merlin led the way to an empty table close to the fire. It was so hot, my fingers stung as the warmth seeped into them.

"Gentleman, what can I get you?" a woman with red hair almost the same colour as my own asked when she stopped beside the table.

I stared at her, but she just smiled down at me, cocking her hip to the side and bending down slightly so her chest bulged out the top of her dress.

Merlin chuckled and rested and elbow on the table, obviously enjoying the view. "Well, little lady, I think us hungry men could use some of that delicious stew I smell cooking, and maybe a few mugs of brew."

"Coming right up," she said with a wink for me. She sauntered away, her hips swaying side to side.

I leaned across the table and glared at Merlin. "What was that?"

Merlin leaned back in his chair, a humorous look on his face. "What was what?" His voice broke into a chuckle.

I narrowed my eyes. "Did you make me a man?"

He burst out laughing, bending over and holding his stomach as his head got perilously close to the table. I wanted to reach out and slam it down. He had the magic to change my appearance and made me a man!? I was definitely not going to be recognized, but still… I didn't want to be a man.

He controlled his laughter finally as the food arrived, but every time he looked at me, he laughed again.

I shook my head and ate my food with a scowl on my face.

Once we finished, he rented a room for us and led the way up the stairs.

"You can take the bed, I'll sleep on the floor," he said as he opened the door to the room, revealing a small but tidy space with a pallet bed piled high with blankets. A small steel grate on the floor let heat up from below and, since the room was just above the fireplace, the room was very warm. Cozy, even.

I had never slept in a room with a man before, but feelings of fondness for the wizard had slunk in. And I knew that was what he was. He was a wizard, one of the most powerful in the country. I could remember that, but not how we met, officially.

I climbed into the bed and under a few blankets. The weight settled me in the space, making me feel less like I needed to run away. My disguise helped but being safe in a locked room with a powerful warlock was better insurance.

"Time for lights out, little sorceress," Merlin said. His words triggered an echo in my mind, launching me back into the memories I had been putting in order.

CHAPTER SEVEN

Ten years earlier.

"You shouldn't be here, little girl," the rough voice of the commander of the Roman army said a moment before his thick hands wrapped around my waist and hoisted me off the top rail of the fence. He lowered me to the ground, where I could no longer see the terrible things that were happening beyond the fence, then he turned me to face him and squatted down in front of me.

My small body shook as I tried to hold back the tears. They escaped anyway, trailing cool streaks down my face. My sandwich forgotten, it fell to the dirt. I wasn't hungry anymore.

"Now," the commander said, using his rough thumb to wipe away the tear trails. "Don't let those men see you crying, or they will think you're weak. Those horses have to be broken in fast, and that means broken hard sometimes."

Commander Artorius straightened to his full height, and I sniffled, wiping the last of the tears from my eyes.

"I knew you were tough," he said, rubbing my head and messing up my red hair.

I kept my head down for the rest of the afternoon, cleaning stalls and filling more water buckets as sweaty horses came back to the barn and new horses left for what I could only assume was training similar to the what the first group of horses received.

By the evening I was exhausted. I walked out of the stable and began the long walk back to the orphanage. The sun was low in the sky, so I stared at the ground as I walked, my eyes too tired to fight the bright rays that threatened to blind me. I turned the last corner and ran straight into a hard chest.

"Oof," I said, falling backward to land in the dirt.

A boy laughed, and I shielded my eyes to see his face. It was Eli, the biggest and meanest boy at the orphanage.

I struggled to my feet and tried to go around him, but he moved back in front of me, blocking my path. "Let me pass," I said quietly.

"Let me pass," he mocked in a false high pitch voice. "Or what?"

I had nothing. I couldn't do anything to this big boy. There was one thing my father taught me, but as I lifted my foot to kick him, his hand grabbed my leg and knocked me down. Then he was on top of me and his fist came down on my nose, hard. Stars flashed in my vision at the force of the blow. Eli got to his feet, spitting on me before he turned and left me there in the dirt.

I had done nothing to provoke him, but I had experience with unprovoked violence since meeting my stepfather. My eyes ran with tears from the shock and pain, but I rolled to my feet. People continued past as I struggled to see my way down home. No-one stopped to check on me, though I could feel a trickle of blood running from my nose. I went through the backyard to the rain barrel used to water the plants in the small garden patch and splashed water onto my face, clearing the blood away. Commander Artorius' words rang through my mind. I didn't want anyone to think I was weak. Perhaps I was alone in the world, but I was strong, and I would make a life for myself here. I would make this my home.

When I was sure the blood had stopped running from my nose, I dried my face on the sleeve of my dress and walked in through the back door of the house.

The smell of dinner floated on the air and I realized I was starving. I dreaded seeing Eli again in the kitchen at dinnertime, but I was too hungry to wait till the morning. Instead, I crossed the house and crept quietly into the kitchen. The boys were all talking loudly and crudely as the older girls set the tables and the small children sat banging their cutlery. I slunk in, my eyes down and slipped into the chair beside Leruis. He wore the same expression as I did, but he winced when he saw my face. I knew my nose was swollen, and my eye was burning so I assumed it was changing colours, too.

"Lily said she warned you," he whispered.

"She did. It was an accident," I replied. I felt a sudden camaraderie with Leruis. He had obviously been the target of Eli to at some point. It explained his careful and quiet demeanor. I didn't want to attract Eli's attention either.

The girls served dinner and no one else seemed to notice my face. Not even Lady Ethel, or perhaps she had noticed but didn't mention it. Either way, I finished my food and went to bed without offering to help clean up. My body was exhausted, and my nose and eye were in too much pain.

I curled up in bed, facing the wall and was asleep before the other children even finished settling in for the night.

The following days were monotonous in their similarity. I got up, I ran out the door, Lady Ethel brought me lunch, which I ate in the barn to stay away from the men working with the horses. By the end of the week, Jag found me while I was eating lunch in the hayloft and said I should come to see the horses. I didn't want to see any more cruelty, but I also didn't want to seem weak, as Commander Artorius had said. So, I followed him down from the loft, clutching my sandwich.

I trailed him nervously out to the gate where I had climbed the first day and Jag lifted me onto the top rail. I squeaked at the speed at which I was tossed up, but he held on until I was steady and then stood beside me, his head just high enough to peek over the top.

The men were all riding their horses in formation. Some carried flags that fluttered along in the wind as they performed loops and circles, sometimes side by side and other times individually. It was like a dance.

"Wow," I said on a soft breath, mesmerized by the beauty of the movements and the way they carried their heads and necks. Most of the horses were dark bay, but one red mare stood out form the rest. Her belly hung low and she moved slower than the rest.

"What is wrong with that mare?" I asked, pointing her out.

Jag chuckled. "She is in foal. Today is her last day under saddle until after she weans her foal. None of these mares were supposed to be bred when we bought them, so the commander is pretty angry about it. We aren't set up for a mare to foal."

My mind sparked with ideas. "The back storage room could be converted to a large stall," I said, stuffing the last of my sandwich into my mouth, then scrambling down intent on doing just that.

"Whoa, little girl, you better check with the Commander before you go turning storerooms into stalls," Jag said.

"And what is going on here?" Lady Ethel said, walking towards us.

"I was just talking to Jag about where we could make a stall for a pregnant mare." My voice was full of excitement which I knew was over the top, but I had never seen a newborn foal and this was one of the greatest opportunities of my life to see it in person.

Lady Ethel turned to Jag, stepping close and placing her hand on his chest. "I didn't know you were so good with children."

Jag blushed, which startled me, but I was too excited to stick around and find out what was going on. "I have to go," I shouted as I took off towards the barn.

I skidded to a stop at the barn door, aware that running through the barn was prohibited unless there was an emergency. So, I walked down the aisle, checking each stall until I found the commander, he was standing beside his big bay horse, while another man rubbed the stallion's leg.

"Will he heal completely?" The commander asked the other man.

"Yes, sir. He will need to be hand walked every day but stay on stall rest for a few weeks."

The commander sighed. "Very well." He looked up and saw me standing at the door, rubbing the stallion's nose. "Morgana, it will be your job to hand walk Fargo every day until he is healed, you understand?"

"Of course, sir," I replied, feeling bad for the big surly stallion. He had bitten one of the army men in the shoulder the day before, tearing the man's skin, but I had never felt threatened by the large horse. If anything, I understood why he was so angry all the time, after seeing the way the horses were treated at the beginning of the riding careers.

"My God, child. Don't stand so near the horse," the other man in the stall said.

I smiled at him and kissed the stallion's nose, reaching up as high as I could. When I couldn't quite reach his itchy spot on his forehead, the stallion lowered his head to encourage me to scratch him.

Commander Artorius, swung the stall door open, disturbing the stallion for a moment, but his big head came back down to press on my chest so I would scratch his ears.

"Don't worry, Leo," the commander said with a chuckle. "They are two peas in a pod, these two. I've never seen anything like it."

The man, Leo, stared, amazed for a moment before saying his farewell and leaving.

"Who was that man?" I asked, closing Fargo's door.

"That was the animal healer. He is very well trained in the arts of healing. If he says the horse will be fine, he will be."

"That's good." I smiled before giving Fargo one last pat. "I have a question for you."

The commander stopped and looked down at me. "What is it?"

"That pregnant mare," I said. "I thought I could set her up a stall in the storage room in the back. There is nothing in there now, but it's much larger and will give her more room to foal."

The commander rubbed his chin. "I supposed as long as you get your other chores done, that will be fine."

A grin split my face. "Thank you, sir." I turned to leave, but the commander spun me back, his gaze racking over my face.

"Who hit you, Morgana?"

I had thought it wasn't so visible under the dirt crusting my face. I had left the dirt to camouflage the bruising that circled beneath my eye and across the bridge of my nose.

"No one, sir. I fell down." My face heated at the lie, but I kept my expression blank. Or so I thought.

"Well, if it happens again, you will let me know who it was that made you fall down and I will take care of it."

I gulped. "Yes, sir."

"Off you go, you have a foaling stall to prepare."

I turned and walked away to find my pitchfork. I would make the best foaling stall any horse had ever seen.

CHAPTER EIGHT

The next few days went by slowly. The mare was happily munching in her stall every time I went past. Jag had told me the signs to watch out for in a mare expecting, but so far all she did was eat and drink... a lot.

I kept busy, cleaning things and tidying until late in the evening, wishing I didn't have to go back to the orphanage and worried I would miss the big moment, but eventually I would drag myself home to have dinner before I starved to death.

Then I would fall into bed and sleep like the dead until morning when I would do it all again.

Each day I walked Fargo around the compound, his big head would hang low, so I could reach him. He would grab bites of grass as we went, but never pulling on the lead or acting up. His leg was swollen, and he had a noticeable limp, but his spirits were good, and I hoped he would be sound again soon.

"Morgana," the commander called to me one day while I was sweeping outside the pregnant mare's stall.

I walked over and he held out his hand. I wasn't sure what he was doing until he set some coins in my palm. My eyes grow large and round. I had never seen so many coins before.

"What?" Then I remembered I was being paid to work. The coins were for Lady Ethel. "Thank you, sir."

He grinned down at me. "Is that mare getting close yet?" he asked.

"I don't know. Perhaps. I'm really anxious but all she does is eat hay."

The commander chuckled. "A watched mare never foals. Why don't you go home early? I'll get these lazy men to do the rest of the chores. The mare is surely not foaling tonight, and you have been staying too late every night for the last while. Don't think I haven't noticed."

Disappointed I said, "Yes, sir," then dragged myself out of the barn and down the street towards the orphanage. I was good enough at making the walk now that I hardly noticed things around me. My mind wandered off to dreamland while my legs carried me home.

Back at the orphanage, I stopped at the parlour expecting to find Lady Ethel, but instead I found the old woman, Mistress Carlyle.

She spotted me before I could back out of the room silently.

"Come in here, child."

I bit my lip and followed her command, stopping before her.

"Who are you?" she asked. "I haven't seen you here all day."

I cleared my throat and squeezed my fingers in an effort to stay calm. The woman was too strict and stern-looking. She made my heart race and my mouth stumble over words.

"I, I am Morgana. Um, Ma'am. I work at the stables."

Her eyes narrowed at me. "So, you don't do any housework? Why are you home now?"

"Uh, the Commander sent me home early because I have been working very hard. He gave me these coins, too." I reached into the pocket of my skirt and pulled out the coins, presenting them to her.

She snatched them out of my hand. "Go bathe, I won't have you stinking up the whole house."

"Yes ma'am," I said, hurrying away. Once I was out of sight, I took a deep breath and leaned against the wall. Where was Lady Ethel? I checked in the kitchen, but only Lily and Breena were in there. I stepped back out before they saw me; I just wanted some quiet time, so climbed the stairs to the bathing room. The water was dingy but cleaner than I was, so I closed the door behind me and stripped out of my dirty dress and got into the cold water. It wasn't freezing, but it was cold enough that goosebumps rose on my flesh.

Back at Uther's castle, the women would sometimes heat the water, so I had experienced warm baths and enjoyed them very much. I dunked my head under the water and soaked for a few moments before rising to breathe. I scrubbed my skin and hair with my hands until my skin was pink, having almost forgotten that my skin was that colour.

Stepping out of the tub, I wrapped myself in a blanket while I dunked my clothes in the tub and scrubbed them, too. The water was black when I was through.

My clothes hung in front of the fire in the bedroom, I lay down on the bed and curled up in a ball beneath the rest of my blankets. I dozed happily, imagining what the new foal would look like. My mind could almost picture his fuzzy nose and thin spiked mane. I had seen a few foals over the years, but never a foal's birth.

After about an hour of lazing about, I got up and pulled on my much cleaner clothes, then took the stairs back down to the kitchen to see if I could help.

Lily and Breena were on their knees, scrubbing the kitchen floor alongside a couple of the toddlers who weren't really cleaning so much as spreading water around.

"Hey, you guys need some help?" I asked.

"Oh, Morgana," Lily said. "Yes, please. We are supposed to start dinner, but Mistress Carlyle said we couldn't until the floor was spotless. She said we would have no dinner if it wasn't finished."

I grabbed a rag and dunked it in the bucket and set to work. "Why is Mistress Carlyle in charge suddenly?" I kept my voice down in case the old woman was still nearby.

"You didn't hear? I guess you wouldn't, being away from the house all the time. Lady Ethel is getting married to an army soldier. She is leaving to start a family of her own." Lily shook her head like it was a tragedy and it might as well have been. Mistress Carlyle was a horrible person and I knew it from the moment I first saw her.

I still couldn't believe that Lady Ethel had left us. I wondered if she was marrying one of the men from the stable. Jag had seemed smitten with her.

"She abandoned us," Breena said. She rarely spoke, but her voice shook with anger. "Well, not all of us. She has taken the little boy with her. I don't even think he had a name."

I knew which one she was talking about. The boy had little ringlets and sticky fingers. He was cute. If she was going to pick one child to take with her, I wasn't surprised it was him. Still, it stung that she left the rest of us to fend for ourselves against the mean old lady.

We finished the floor and started on dinner. There wasn't time to cook the meat before dinner, so we just made a broth and bread, but it was better than going to bed hungry.

"There will be no talking," Mistress Carlyle said, blowing out the lamp and closing the door. It was a far cry from the usual story before bed, but I hoped that she would relax once she saw that we were all well behaved.

My hope was in vain.

By the end of the week, we had missed more meals than eaten and I began to struggle to keep up with my chores.

The mare still hadn't foaled, and I was exhausted from going home and doing more chores at the house before bed. I hadn't seen Lady Ethel in days but finally heard gossip that Jag had married a pretty young woman. I knew then it was her. Jag had taken her from us and left us with the witch.

One day when I was out walking Fargo, I crossed the lane just as Jag rode up on his gelding. He was a thick gelding, but not as solid as Fargo. Still, he suited the large bearded man and looked like a sturdy mount.

"Hey, Morgana, I haven't seen you around much." It's possible I had been avoiding him. Turning corners when I saw him coming and hiding if he came through the barn.

"I've been here," I said, walking on and not looking back.

"Wait," he said from behind me, but I didn't. The sound of his boots hitting the ground and following me made me look over my shoulder. Sure enough, he was leading his horse, trying to catch up to me.

"Hold on, Fargo," I whispered. The big stallion stopped and ate a few bites of grass, happy to chew that while I talked to the army man.

"Are you avoiding me?" Jag asked, his thick beard hiding most of his face.

"No."

"Are you sure, because I saw you duck down behind a stall wall when I came in the barn yesterday."

I thought for sure he hadn't seen me. I didn't reply since it wasn't a question.

"Tell me why you are avoiding me." He crouched down in front of me, so we were face to face, and I had nowhere else to go.

"You stole her from us," I whispered. I hadn't wanted to confess, but I felt like Jag and I were friends and he should know what he did.

"Ethel?" he asked surprised.

"Yes! And now we have a mean old lady who makes us work twice as hard and only lets us eat half as much. I haven't eaten in two days and I can barely stand." Tears sprung to my eyes. The pain and sorrow of losing someone else came pouring out.

"Aw. I'm sorry, little girl." He scooped me up and hugged me. His thick arms were nearly as wide as I was, and I felt safe there wrapped up in his embrace. I hadn't realized how much I had become friends with the army men until after that day when they took turns giving me something for lunch: Some bread or cheese, a piece of fruit or a bowl of stew. I didn't go hungry after that, but some others at the orphanage did, so I began to keep a little of the food and take it home, giving it to whoever needed it the most.

On the fourth day of doing that, I was walking home with a few slices of bread tucked in my pocket when I was stopped by Eli and two other boys from the orphanage just as I rounded a stone wall that circled a house on the street corner.

"Come on, hand it over," Eli said, his grip on my arm brutal. I struggled to get away, but he was too much bigger than me.

"I don't know what you're talking about," I said. Wriggling and tugging against his grip.

"Sure, you do. Those army men are giving you food and I want it. So, hand it over."

When I didn't, he jerked his arm back, his big fist tight and his expression angry. I turned away to protect my face, so his fist slammed into my temple. I dropped, stunned and dazed. The world was spinning, and lights flashed in my eyes. I couldn't catch myself, so when he dropped me, I fell to the dirt, my already battered head bouncing off the ground.

"Search her," I heard Eli say, and then hands roamed over me as I writhed in pain until they found the bread tucked in my pocket. I groaned and tried to get up, but a heavy boot kicked me in the stomach. Something snapped, and the air rushed out of my lungs. I curled up, trying to get some air and protect myself, but it was no use. The boot came at my face and cracked right into my cheek. The hot copper taste of blood pooled in my mouth, then ran down my cheek to the ground beneath me, mixing with the tears that further blocked my vision.

"That'll teach you to hold out on me. I'll see you tomorrow." Eli's voice held laughter as if it were all a big joke. The rest of the boys laughed and joked as they strode away.

I lay where I was for a long time. Until long after the sun had set, and the sky grew dark. Even after the owl began to sing his haunting nighttime song. A fog rolled off the water and up through the city, making everything look eerie. The whoosh of flapping wings startled my eyes open a moment after they slid closed, and I glanced up into the tree in time to see a white owl land there and stare down at me with wide blinking eyes.

I reached up to my neck and ran my thumb and finger over the warm pendant there. It always stayed hidden beneath my clothes, but right now I felt too far from my mother and sisters. I was alone, broken in the dirt, and knew no one would come to help me.

"Mother," I rasped, cleared my throat and tried again. "Mother, please help me."

It might have been my addled mind from the heavy blows my head had taken, but I swore I saw my mother's face in the fog. She mouthed the words, "For I am not worthy."

The pain in my chest eased. The smell of rain in spring and honeysuckle floated through the air. Soon, the pain vanished, as did the throbbing in my face and head. I took a deep breath, filling my lungs with cool night air that revived my mind, making me feel whole again.

I pushed up to a sitting, leaning back against the stone wall. "What just happened?" I muttered. The owl hooted from the tree and then flew on his way, disappearing in the fog.

I brought my hand up to my swollen cheek, but it was normal now. No swelling or pain.

Whatever had just happened, it was definitely magic. Nothing else could have healed me so fast. If it was magic, I could never tell a soul, or I would be dead. Everyone knew that magic was dangerous and punishable by death.

CHAPTER NINE

Present

I woke to find the room empty. Merlin's makeshift bed still lay on the floor, vacant except for a note. It said, "There is a bath across the hall. Then come down for breakfast."

I gave myself a sniff, then pulled open the door and peeked my head out. Across the hall was another closed door, with no sign to indicate it was a bathing room. I stepped out fully and closed the door behind me, then lifted my hand and knocked on the door across the hall.

After a long moment, when nobody answered, I pushed the door open and was relieved to see a large bathtub full of clear water. I quickly pulled off my dirty and wrinkled clothes and slipped into the water. It was cold, but I said the word that came as naturally as breathing "Byrne." The small flame flickered to life beneath the surface of the water and I leaned back, enjoying the way the water warmed. That small comfort was short-lived, though, when the thought of the last time I had used the magic flooded in. The screams of the people as the building came down on them. The blood. The horror.

A shiver raced down my spine as that thought led to what happened last time I sat in a tub of heated water. The loss of Copper was still fresh, too. I quickly dunked my head under the water, scrubbing my locks, then surfaced and rose, stepping out of the water and crushing the magic flames beneath my heel.

I grabbed a cloth and dried myself, then pulled on my clothes and went downstairs to find Merlin. Being alone with my memories wasn't pleasing.

I found the wizard sitting at a table with a beautiful woman. Her hair was long and blonde; in fact, her colouring matched Paxton's. That was another painful memory, and I brushed it aside as I moved through the room and pulled out a chair at the table where they sat.

Merlin's face curled into a grin. "There you are."

"Here I am," I said leaning back in the chair and studying the pair of them. A fit of sudden jealousy lashed up from somewhere inside me. I had no time to inspect the emotion before the blonde woman rose and left.

"What's the matter?" Merlin asked.

"Nothing. I'm sorry," I replied.

"All right," he said, his face still studying mine. "Would you like some breakfast before we go?"

"Where is it we're going?"

Merlin leaned in closer to me across the table. "The Isle of Man."

I narrowed my eyes at him. "That's not a real place. It's a myth."

Merlin leaned back and waved to a woman in an apron and she came over to our table, so I had to wait to press him further.

"Two breakfasts, please." He said it with a grin and the woman blushed, dropping her eyes to the floor.

"Of course, sir. Sir." She said the last looking at me. I had almost forgotten that the people here thought I was a man. She hurried away, and I went back to my inquisition.

"The Isle of Man isn't real," I repeated.

"Of course, it is. It's as real as you and I. It's as real as Avalon."

I scoffed. "Avalon is only partially real." Or at least it was before I got to it. Most of it had to have been magic.

"You are correct, I suppose. Let's say it's as real as your horse."

That was almost a punch in the gut. My poor Copper. I didn't know how to be happy to have him back when he was only really a product of magic.

The woman set our plates of food down and the conversation died. The warm bread and gooey eggs were perfect, warming me from the inside. I ate it all and sipped some ale, although I didn't like the taste, so mostly avoided it.

"Are you ready to get back on the road?" Merlin asked, dropping some coins on the table.

"I guess. I wish it weren't so cold out though."

"Well, we are in luck, because an early thaw arrived overnight, lessening the cold quite a bit. Let's go get the horses and enjoy the break while we can."

I followed Merlin's broad back through the inn and around back to the stable. He was right; it was much milder today. The sun even shone warmly.

Merlin slid open the stable door and the rush of moist air scented heavily with horses and hay met my nose.

Copper nickered at me as he used to do, and it pulled a grin to my face. He and Sara were side by side, standing together, though the stall wall divided them. Sara had a mouth full of hay and was munching happily.

A small boy came out from a stall further down and startled when he saw us.

"I'm so sorry, did you want me to get them saddled?"

"Not mine, he will go without." I glanced at Merlin who also shook his head.

"I can saddle my own horse. Here is a coin for taking such good care of them." He handed the boy a coin, which disappeared into his small pocket.

"The chestnut wouldn't eat the hay, sir. I tried to convince him, but he turned up his nose."

"Oh, I'm sorry, yes, I should have mentioned the horse only eats while out travelling," Merlin said in response to the boy.

I was thankful he answered because I was too shocked to even think. Copper no longer ate?

The boy shrugged and wandered off.

Sighing, I opened Copper's stall door and stepped inside. His soft nose touched my cheek and his warm breath sent a shiver down my spine. "Silly horse." I stroked his forehead until Merlin was ready to go.

We mounted our horses and left the city without incident. The sun was blinding off the snow but felt amazing on my face, reminding me of the memory I had gone through while I was asleep.

"So, I had magic when I was little?" I asked Merlin, startling him out of whatever he was thinking so hard about.

"Oh, yes. Your mother brought forth your magic early with the necklace. You would have had magic before long now anyway since you were destined to, but your mum was quick-thinking and gave you the only gift that would have saved you."

"Would I have died when that bully and his friends beat me up?" I asked. I had been beaten, but I hadn't thought I was near death.

"Oh, you're only there. Continue in your remembering, girl. We can discuss it later." Merlin began to hum a soft tune, and I disappeared into my memories again.

CHAPTER TEN

Ten years earlier.

I entered the house that night and went straight to the bedroom. My body was whole, but exhausted, as though the magic had stolen all the energy from my body.

I regretted losing the bread for the children, particularly Leruis, who had been ill and had lost even more weight than the rest of us with the new restricted diet, thanks to the evil old hag that was now running the orphanage.

My pay from the stables, plus generous donations from various wealthy citizens of the city, more than covered the cost of feeding us twice a day, but the Mistress Carlyle said we should be thankful for what we had. She was thankful for her fancy new clothes, I could tell.

I was left to sleep, thankfully, though that meant I had no dinner. I needed the sleep more, so when I woke in the morning before the sun rose, I felt much better.

My feet hit the floor and I raced down the stairs, almost forgetting about the trauma of the day before until I ran into the kitchen and came face to face with Eli.

His expression morphed from hatred to one of shock and then one of complete contempt. His face turned red and his fists clenched. He looked as though he was about to tell everyone that I was a sorceress when the gears in his tiny mind ground together and he realized he would have to admit to beating me if he wanted to tell on me. A grin tried to form on my lips, but I bit it back. No reason to taunt my tormentor.

"Have a good day," I said, slipping past him and out the back door of the house. I broke into a sprint, my legs flying over the ground so fast I was on the verge of falling the whole way to the stables.

I skidded to a stop at the door, thankful I made it.

As my eyes adjusted to the dim stable, I could make out several men standing around the back storage room; the one I had converted into a foaling stall.

I strode forward, then tugged on sleeves until one soldier lifted me to his shoulder so I could see. The mare was on her side, heaving, and straining, but a tiny pair of hooves was the only thing visible from behind her.

"Oh wow," I whispered and the soldier whose shoulder I perched on chuckled along with a few others who were also watching the birth of a new life.

It wasn't long until the rest of the new foal slid from the mare and thrashed awkwardly until he was free of the sac that had contained him inside his dam. The little colt nickered and so did the mare. The pair of them nickering back and forth as though in conversation was a beautiful and touching moment.

A few tears escaped from my eyes, but I quickly wiped them away. One by one the soldiers went back to their duties, and I knew I had to as well. The soldier set me on my feet at the door to the stall, and I peered at the wet and sticky foal as his mother rose to her feet and began licking his head and neck with her wide tongue.

"Did you get to see the birth as you wished?" Commander Artorius asked from behind me.

"I'm sorry sir, I'll get to work," I said, startled. The rest of the men were grooming their horses while I stood around doing nothing.

"It's all right Morgana, it's a special day. What's your colt's name?" he asked.

"My colt, sir?"

"Yes, well, as I said, we have little use for a young colt here, but if you take care of him, I suppose he could live in that small stall in the hay barn once he is weaned from his mother."

"Of course, I will take care of him, sir," I said nearly leaping out of my skin.

"Good," he replied with a grin. "What is this beast's name?"

I glanced back at the sticky colt, his coat was chestnut like his mothers, except it shone in the dark. "Copper."

The commander chuckled. "A fine name. Now you better get to your chores. Those horses want some hay and water before they work this morning."

"Yes, sir, of course." I hurried off and grabbed my pitchfork, before beginning the climb to the loft.

Nearly halfway up, a strong pair of arms peeled me off the ladder and set me back on my feet. "I'll throw it down, Morgana, or you'll be there all day. You feed those hungry beasts."

"Thank you, Jag," I said, running off to wait at the bottom of the chute. As the hay fell, I scooped it up and shoved some in each stall, moving with a spring in my step I had never had before. I had my own horse. Copper. The most beautiful colt in all of Briton.

Once I had the horses fed and watered, I went back to staring at Copper. He was still laying down in much the same place he had been. But now his mother was nosing and nudging him as though she was concerned.

"What's the matter, lady?" I asked.

The little copper colt attempted to unfold his legs, but they were stuck in a bent shape at the knees and he could only raise his hindquarters before falling back to the straw.

"Oh, no." I turned and raced off to find the Commander. He was out riding Fargo in the fenced riding school with the rest of the men, so I climbed to the top of the gate and swung my legs over the side. When I caught the commander's eye, I waved him towards me. Fargo nickered as he noticed me, too, and rested his head in my lap when the commander stopped in front of me.

"Commander, I don't think Copper can stand. His legs are bent."

The commander's face fell into a frown. "I'm so sorry, Morgana. I should have waited to give him to you until I was sure he would live. Some foal's legs are just too poor, and they die. I can end his suffering as soon as we are done here."

"No!" I yelled, startling the commander and Fargo. "I mean, I'll help him, Commander Artorius. I can do it. I promise."

I turned and climbed down the gate and was gone before he could stop me. No one would kill Copper.

I opened the stall door, and the mare pinned her ears at me. I had spent little time with her as my other duties took up most of the day, but I kept a steady voice and moved slowly.

"It's okay, lady, I'm just going to help your little guy." No one was around, all the soldiers out training their horses, so I hoped I didn't get trampled by an angry broodmare. I raised my hand and let her touch her nose to my palm, wishing I had treats for her. If she could just trust me a little, I could help her colt.

I remembered the magic of the day before -- the way it healed my face and ribs -- and wondered if I could heal Copper the same way. Though I didn't really know how I had done it before. The mare's ears came forward and her soft nose nuzzled my palm.

I sighed with relief. Then stepped towards the little chestnut foal, his chin rested on his legs and his mound of twisted chin whiskers looked silly on such a small face.

"Hello there, little one," I said. I was honestly not much bigger than he was, but I had never seen such a small horse in my life. His hooves were no bigger than the palm of my hand and I was pretty sure my legs were longer than his. I sat down in the hay beside his head and he nickered softly to me.

I stroked his forehead as his eyes slid shut. He seemed weak and tired. Probably not the way a foal should be acting. Everything I knew about young animals was that they were bouncy and silly and then would sleep a lot, but Copper hadn't even made it to his feet yet, so he probably hadn't eaten yet either.

I ran my hands down his neck and across his shoulders to his legs. I tried to straighten them out, but they were tight at his knees. The bend in his leg too severe. I took my hands away and retrieved my mother's necklace from beneath my collar before removing it and placing it around the young foal's neck instead.

When nothing happened, I pressed my hand to the smooth golden owl, pushing it against the colt's neck, then I said some words that came quietly to my mind like a whisper on the wind. "Heal this horse for I am not worthy." A soft glow came from the owl, peeking between my fingers and from around my hand. It warmed to nearly burning, and I dropped my hand away. A moment later the glow stopped, and the colt jumped to his feet, standing proud and tall for all to see.

A gasp alerted me to a presence behind me.

"Oh child," Lady Ethel said, from her place standing beside an equally shocked Jag. "What have you done?"

"Nothing!" I cried. "He was fine, I just overreacted before."

Copper had made his way to his mother and was suckling happily.

"Morgana," Jag's voice was stern but sad. "We just watched you. Whatever you did, it wasn't normal."

"Please! You can't tell anyone! I promise I'll never do it again." Tears rolled down my cheeks, and I stumbled to the stall door and threw myself at the feet of the people who had been so kind to me. I repaid their kindness by using magic and destroying myself. They would burn me in the town square, along with the other evildoers.

They said nothing for a long moment. I looked up and realized they were staring at each other.

"Morgana, get off the ground," Lady Ethel said. "We won't tell anyone, except..."

Jag sighed. "Except an old friend of mine who can help you. But you must never use magic anywhere except where he says it's safe. Do you understand?"

"Yes, of course!" I said rising and dusting the dirt off my knees. "I'll never use it again."

Jag scooped me up and held me in his arms. "Foolish girl. I didn't say to never use it again," his voice was low and made only for my ears. "I said not except where my friend says it's safe."

"Who's your friend?" I asked, sniffling.

Jag leaned in even closer until his mouth was just beside my ear. "His name is Merlin."

CHAPTER ELEVEN

Present

I lifted my head and turned to look at Merlin. His eyes were closed, and he was slouched in the saddle as his grey mare marched on as though she were possessed. Copper was longer-legged than the mare, but he had been meeting her stride all day as if he hoped she would notice him. The grey mare barely batted an ear in his direction, but that didn't dissuade the silly chestnut gelding.

I went back to studying Merlin, but when I looked up his eyes were open, and he was gazing at me.

"Have you reached my grand entrance to your life yet?"

I snorted a laugh. "Just about. I saved Copper's life once before." My hand slid down Copper's neck to scratch his whither.

"Once before?" Merlin chuckled. "Oh child, you have been saving that horse for his whole life. You best keep going. You are just getting to the best part."

I shook my head, but let the memories flood back in.

CHAPTER TWELVE

Ten years earlier

True to their words, Ethel and Jag kept my secret and a full week passed. Eli was either too frightened to approach me again, or he was planning something. Either way, I had a reprieve from him, and I used it to my full advantage.

"Morgana, how do you keep bringing all this food home?" Leruis asked one night when I was stuffing him full of a bun with shaved ham on it.

"The men don't mind giving me some of their extra food. They get fed much better than we do." I grinned down at him. His illness relapsed, and he was again bed-ridden. The other girls took good care of him, but he needed food to sustain him.

Once he had eaten as much as he could, I split the rest in two and gave it to the youngest two children who had taken to waiting outside the bedroom door to get whatever scraps were left. My stomach was sick with the fact they were acting more like stray dogs than children now, but there was little I could do.

"What do you think you're doing?" Mistress Carlyle's harsh voice called out behind me as I walked towards the girl's bedroom.

I turned and looked at the old woman. She used a cane to walk now but often used it to remind children of their manners, too.

"I was just going to lie down for a few minutes, ma'am," I said dropping my eyes to the floor.

"Oh, no. You can go help the boys clean the yard since you are so set on doing a man's work. I expect you to work until bedtime to make up for your laziness. No dinner for you."

I nodded and stepped forward, planning to go around her to go down the stairs, but she blocked the way, much as Eli had when I had attempted to get past him.

"Do you think you are special and should deserve special privileges?" she croaked right beside my ear.

"No, ma'am," I said.

Her cane lashed out so fast I didn't expect it. I hit me hard in the ribs and a now-familiar crack sound proceeded all the air rushing out of my lungs. I dropped like a stone, gasping for breath.

"Don't be so dramatic, Morgana. Get to work or I'll give you something to cry about."

I hadn't been crying. My ability to hold back tears was something of a talent at this point, but I still couldn't gather air and my brain started to panic.

I dragged myself to my feet, gasping and coughing, then past her and started down the stairs, but the hall went grey and then black.

My eyes opened in the dark, the sound of soft snoring surrounded me, comforting and familiar. I tipped my face toward the window and found the moon was still hanging high in the night sky, but the movement sent a sharp stab of pain through my neck and shoulders. The gasp that followed had me clutching my ribs where Mistress Carlyle had whacked me with her cane.

My hand immediately rose to the owl necklace that hung at my neck, warm against my skin. Before I could do anything to ease my pain, the memory of Lady Ethel and Jag's word rang through my memory.

Jag said not to use magic again until his friend arrived to help me.

So, instead, I forced my body off my pallet bed and tiptoed through the house and out the back door.

I was winded by the time I made it there but pushed forward at a slow hobbling pace. I wanted to see Copper and make sure he was okay. My broken body would be no use at work today but knew that Commander Artorius wouldn't fire me from my job.

"I fell down the stairs," I whispered as I rounded the first corner on my way towards the stables. "I tripped on the stairs." That didn't sound convincing either. I definitely fell down the stairs, if the bruising all over my body was any indication, but the crack to my ribs was the cause, not clumsy feet.

I stopped, leaned against the side of a stone building and took some deep, slow breaths. The street was empty except for the occasional stray dog.

I slid down to sit on the ground. I could rest for a moment and then I would go see Copper. My eyes were heavy, but I fought them to stay open. They must have slid shut for a moment because suddenly a man was crouched in front of me. His dark hair shone in the moonlight as though he wore a halo.

"Angel?" I asked, ready to welcome my afterlife. The man's twinkling eyes settled the anxiety that mixed with the exhaustion.

"No, child. I fear you may think of me as the devil, instead." He grinned and I couldn't help but grin back as my eyes tried to slide shut again. "Now, now, there will be no time for sleeping. I'd say you are quite close to the edge. Let's just pull you back a bit so we can go somewhere safe."

The man looked up and down the street, then his hand reached out and his finger touched my forehead. My eyes slammed shut just as a spark lit from behind my eyelids, blowing up like a fire on dry leaves. My body jolted, and the pain vanished as though it had never been there. I sighed and relaxed back against the stone wall.

"Not quite done yet, but I think it will keep you with us long enough." Strong arms scooped me up off the ground and carried me easily through the city. My eyes would sag open from time to time and glimpse a building or the man's shadowed face. He looked nice, like a kind man. Like my father.

"Magic?" my voice was barely a whisper and the effort to say that one word took nearly everything I had.

"Shh, it's not safe here."

He walked along for several minutes or it could have been hours before he glanced down at me once and grinned. "Almost there now. Hang on."

I let my eyes slip shut again, trusting the magic man not to hurt me. My dreams were filled with the man and I riding across the country. I was aboard Copper, and he was riding a grey mare. Though I was much older, my hair was just as fiery red. Copper was stunning, his neck arched as he pranced along. The look on my face was one of happiness and that was reassuring for some reason. When I woke, I reflected on the dream and forced my hand up to hold the golden owl at my neck. Maybe it hadn't been a dream, but a premonition. I hoped it was. I wanted nothing more than to ride through the country with Copper.

The man stopped at a door and shifted me so he could open it. Once through the door, he kicked it shut behind him and lay me down on a long table that sat in the middle of the kitchen. I felt exposed and uncomfortable, but he quickly threw a blanket over me and tucked another under my head.

"There now, just give me a minute and we can get you healed up, good as new."

He disappeared into another room and when he returned, he held a leather-bound book. His long strides brought him back to stand beside me.

"Now, I believe you have already figured out you can heal, thanks to your mother's pendant. Are you able to do anything else?"

I shook my head. It made my vision blurry a bit, but there was no pain. I closed my eyes, but the man spoke again.

"All right, well, let's see you heal yourself, then."

I opened my eyes and looked up at him. The room seemed to have gotten foggy or maybe it was my vision. "I can't. Jag said." I whispered before closing my eyes again. No more seeing. It was too weird.

"It's now or never, girl." The words were off the cuff as if he didn't care, but when I peeled open my eyes I saw his imploring look. He wanted me to heal myself.

I closed my eyes again and the vision of me riding Copper across a clover field, his tail high and my hands wrapped up in his long ginger mane made me gasp. At that moment, I knew that it was my future. I couldn't say how I knew, but it was a surety. Unless I didn't use my magic today to heal the damage my body had sustained.

I couldn't force my eyes open, but I raised my hand to my neck, where I felt the warmth of my mother's necklace. It heated quickly in my fist and I said the words I had used to heal Copper.

"Heal me, for I am not worthy." The warmth of the owl burst into a fevered heat that singed my palm. My back arched off the table as the soft smell of ripe apples drifted up to my nose, stinging the sensitive tissues there. The heavy feeling drifted, and I began to breathe easier. My mind cleared and when I opened my eyes, so did the room. It was a tidy home, with a large hearth and stools surrounding the table I lay on.

"Can I sleep now?" I asked, rolling onto my side, which no longer hurt.

A hand set down gently on my head and smoothed back my hair, which I realized was sticky with sweat.

"Yes, child. Sleep now." The voice held a bit of humour, which eased my mind, and I fell into a peaceful sleep. One with dreams of glittering horses and open meadows of sweet clover.

CHAPTER THIRTEEN

I woke in the same place. Wrapped up in a heavy blanket on the kitchen table across from the hearth which blazed with fire, despite it still being summer. The heat felt good, and I was hesitant to move until the man's voice said, "Ah, there you are."

His face moved into my line of view and his mouth was pulled up into a big grin. I studied him for a moment. The creases around his eyes put him nearly old enough to be my father, but there was a lightness to him. A youthfulness that most adults didn't possess.

"Who are you?" I asked, my voice clear.

The man straightened. "Merlin, at your service." He bowed at the waist but kept his twinkling eyes on me.

"Okay," I said, confused.

"I'm the wizard that will train you to use your magic safely."

"Jag sent you?" I asked.

"No. I was always meant to come. He was just the inciting character who brought us together."

I squinted at him. "What does that mean?"

"It means, in the timeline of you and I, we were meant to meet. But it had to be at the right time as predestined by natural forces. It couldn't be rushed. Though I may have helped it along a tiny bit here and there." He held out his thumb and forefinger, showing the tiny bit he helped our destiny.

I glanced away, noticing the sun high in the sky out the window. "I have to get to work," I said, throwing the blanket off.

"Jag has already covered for you. You might as well enjoy the quiet time."

"If I don't work, Mistress Carlyle will be angry." My cheeks blushed at the memory of what happened when you disappointed Mistress Carlyle. I finished pushing the blanket off and swung up to sit on the side of the table.

"Look, Morgana. You are going to have to figure out a way to be here for a few hours a day. You can't wander around with that much power and no sense of how to use it properly. Bad things could happen. Terrible things."

A sudden image of the whole city on fire flashed into my mind. I saw women and children running and screaming while every structure had flames licking up the sides including the stables.

"Okay," I said.

"Oh, well, that was easier than I was expecting," Merlin grinned. "Most children hate studies."

I crinkled my nose. "Yes, well. I don't imagine most children have magic."

"You are correct. It is very few who have the ability to use magic and it's just as well. Most never have the power you already possess, thankfully. You will be a problem, I can tell."

I rolled my eyes. "I'm never a problem."

He scoffed. "How many people have already seen you use magic or seen the results of that magic?"

I looked down. All right, he had a point.

"Okay. Enough for today. Go visit your little horse and then come back here for dinner. You will have to keep living at the orphanage, but I'll ensure your Mistress Carlyle doesn't miss you... or touch you ever again."

The last part was spoken with a cut to the words. I didn't doubt he would make sure I was safe from the old woman, though it was Eli I was more worried about. I didn't bring that up since I would have to admit the boy already knew I had magic. He was keeping my secret for now and hadn't bothered me since the last time when I healed myself, so I would just hope he stayed out of my way and I would stay out of his.

When I left Merlin's cottage, I glanced around until I found the tall church steeple. I knew it wasn't far from the stables, so headed that way through the city. I hadn't had time to explore much of the city past my route to the stables and back to the orphanage, but it was a beautiful day. The air was crisp as the summer was waning, but it was still perfectly mild and wonderful for walking. I wasn't looking forward to another winter near the shore. The wind coming off the water would burn on my cheeks and the snow would gather, making walking much harder.

I passed the orphanage. The boys were behind the building chopping wood. The big house would need a lot of that for the coming winter. Once I was past home, I was in familiar territory again, so I broke into a run and careened through the city like my tail was on fire. I ran so fast I didn't even notice when I passed Lady Ethel until she called out from behind me.

"Morgana?"

I slid to a halt and turned to see Lady Ethel's friendly face. She held the hand of the little toddler boy who had once lived at the orphanage. He looked much brighter than when I had last seen him, and as though he had grown a few inches.

"Hello," I said.

"You are looking better. Jag said you had a little mishap."

"Yes. I'm all better now, thank you. I met Jag's friend, and he helped me."

Lady Ethel smiled. "That's terrific news. Now, remember to be careful."

"Of course," I said smiling brightly at her.

Lady Ethel surprised me by wrapping her arms around me. The little toddler at her side wrapped his arms around my thigh and we all laughed.

"I'd better get home. See you soon, Morgana."

"Thank you," I said before turning and walking the rest of the way to the stable. Inside some men moved about, grooming or tacking horses, but I passed them all and slipped into the stall at the very back.

A soft nicker greeted me, and I sat down in the fresh hay someone had put down. I was also glad to find someone had filled the water bucket and manger. Copper strolled over to me as though I were just an option. He was already a bold colt: fearless and proud.

"Hey there, trouble," I said as he sniffed my hair. I reached up and stroke his soft coat, then ran my fingers through his short mane that stood on end.

Then he spun lightening quick and dashed back to his mother, stopping short but still colliding with her side. She grunted but continued munching her hay while Copper ran laps around the stall, bucking and squealing. Laughter bubbled up and out. I couldn't help myself. He was silly and clumsy, but so agile, too.

"He'll be a handful," the deep voice of Commander Artorius said with a chuckle.

I jumped to my feet. "I'm sorry, I should be working, I just wanted to see him."

"Jag said you were sick and that you needed a day or two off. Are you feeling better?"

"Oh, yes, sir. I'm sorry. It was just a misunderstanding. I'll get back to my chores." I opened the latch on the stall, but the commander didn't move out of the way so I could exit.

"Why don't you just take the day and relax. The men have been getting lazy not having to do their own chores. A day of work will keep them humble. Besides, you better teach that colt to lead. He decided not to follow his mother out to the paddock last night and it took three men to herd him back in. His poor dam nearly had a heart attack when the silly thing took off on her."

"I'm sorry. I'll do that right now. He won't be any more trouble, I promise."

The commander laughed. "Don't worry so much, Morgana. I've spent too many years with horses to expect a colt to be anything short of a handful." He passed me a small rope halter and lead then turned and left me to my task.

I spent the better part of the afternoon, just getting the halter on the colt. Eventually, he lay down to have a nap, and I stuffed his face into the halter before he had time to jump back up.

As soon as it was tied though, the rodeo began. Copper tossed his head and threw himself at his dam. He rubbed his nose on her belly, making her annoyed enough to pin her ears at him. Then he came back to me and tried rubbing it off on my back. When that didn't work, he finally settled and stood beside me while I scratched his nose and around his ears. All the places the unnatural material touched his soft fur.

"I know you don't like it, boy, but you have to be a good horse, or they won't let me keep you." He stood beside me quietly while I attached the rope to his halter.

Then I took a step away and gave a little tug. He took a step forward, and I nearly melted at his intelligence a moment before he leapt backward, tearing the rope from my hand and running back to his mother. The rope was short, only as long as my forearm and made to be left on as a catch strap, so I decided that was enough for one day and backed out of the stall, waving to Copper. He nickered once as I re-latched the door. I peeked over and he was there, staring at me.

He rested his chin on the stall door and his fuzzy whiskers were too good to resist, so I kissed his nose, then walked out of the stable.

The sun was much lower than I expected, so I jogged back the way I had come. When I passed the orphanage, the children were all going inside for dinner, but I kept going, making my way by memory back to Merlin's cottage.

Some people were out walking the streets, enjoying the end of the summer as winter would come soon. I passed them, watching out for men on horseback and carriages that were travelling through the city.

As the sun lowered below the horizon, I caught sight of the cozy cottage. Its roof was peaked taller than most of the surrounding homes and a garden of bright red flowers bloomed out front despite the late season.

I crossed the street and knocked on the door.

"Just a second," Merlin's voice came from beyond the door.

A moment later, the door swung open to reveal the wizard dressed all in dark clothes that made his features more pronounced. He ushered me inside and swung the door closed behind me. I turned to face him, and he held out his closed fist as if it held something important.

Without speaking, he uncurled one finger at a time until he revealed a glowing ball. It hovered over his palm like a cloud but sent off tiny sparks that sizzled in the air before disappearing.

I took a step back. "What is that?"

The wizard grinned and tossed the ball up into the air where it exploded into a million sparks that rained down around us. Some landed on me, but they didn't burn, they just fizzled out and vanished.

"That is magic," Merlin said with a wide grin. "And that is what I will teach you here."

CHAPTER FOURTEEN

Present.

The horses had been climbing for nearly an hour. The terrain was rougher than any I had seen, but I had never been this far northwest. Rocks threatened to give way beneath our horses' feet, but neither horse was willing to slow the pace. The sky was growing dark and we would have to stop for the night soon, but I had seen little sign of civilization in the past few hours. The winter breeze that had been mild, was now bitter and damp, licking at my exposed skin like the end of a whip.

"Merlin!" I called ahead. His mare had insisted on being out front, so Copper finally conceded her the lead.

The wizard spun in his saddle to look at me. "What is it?"

"We can't exactly sleep outside on this mountain. You have a plan, don't you?"

The man grinned. "Of course, I do. I always have a plan, remember?" The wind whipped his hair around like shrubs in a hurricane. But I didn't, in fact, remember that he always had a plan. I remembered weird fragments until I put them in order, and I was still hesitant to trust anything completely. He could have used magic to put these thoughts in my mind.

At that moment though, we reached the top of the mountain. Merlin pulled his mare to a halt and let Copper and I catch up, stopping beside him and his gray mare.

Before us was the sight of stark, white snow reaching down to the ocean. The snow was cast slightly pink by the setting sun, but the skyline stretched out as if it was unending. The blue ocean touched the horizon, which exploded into bright red and pink, fading into purple as it rose into the sky. A few stars twinkled above us; the rest washed out by the fading daylight.

"Whoa," I whispered.

Merlin chuckled but kept his eyes locked on the bottom of the rocky hill where a cozy city hugged the shore.

"It will be dark before we reach the city," I said, worried about the terrain in the dark.

"We better get a move on then." Merlin pushed his mare forward and Copper eagerly followed behind.

The descent was as treacherous as I had assumed it would be. The snow and ice coated the slick rocks, making the horses slip more than once, but both horses were sure-footed, and I trusted Copper to keep us out of trouble. I clutched his mane but leaned back to keep my center above his.

By the time we reached the bottom, my legs were shaking from gripping so tightly, and the sky was pitch black except for the stars that shone down. Ahead, the grey mare almost glowed in the moonlight. She was stunning in the daylight, but now she shone with a radiance that suggested she was never of this earth to begin with. Even the white snow paled in comparison to her bright coat.

Copper shook his head as if he could hear my thoughts and agreed with them. I giggled and stroked his neck as we made our way into the city. The damp wind died down, but was still bitter, so I was glad when Merlin stopped in front of an inn and slid from his horse's back.

My legs were uncooperative, but eventually, I landed in a heap beside Copper, to my embarrassment. Merlin didn't seem to notice, though, as he led Sara to the stable beside the inn. Copper followed, and I awkwardly followed him on numb legs.

Inside it was warm and damp with the heat of the animals. A tall thin man took Sara and promised to care for them after Merlin handed him some coins.

Then Merlin swung his arm over my shoulders and led me to the door of the inn. The warmth of being tucked into his side was comforting. I was exhausted from so much riding and my mind struggled to stay in the present, intent on returning to the past to put the rest of the missing pieces in place.

"Wait, shouldn't you make me a man again," I asked, already half asleep in the warmth of Merlin's closeness.

"Nah," Merlin replied. "I'm sure no one this far north has heard of your mishap yet."

In my haze, Merlin ushered me up a set of stairs and into a cozy room. The bed took up most of the room and smelled musty, but I collapsed on it, kicking my boots off with my feet since I was too tired to reach for them. Then I crawled to the top of the bed and curled up under the covers, leaving my tiger skin wrapped around me. I shivered and shook but drifted off anyway. My mind stayed thankfully blank the rest of the night. Giving me a reprieve from my past.

I woke, overly hot and wrapped up in a pair of arms. A body was nestled in beside me and I didn't immediately remember where I was; I tumbled out of the low bed and onto the floor before I processed that I was even awake.

I pushed myself up and glared at the stranger in my bed only to realize it was Merlin and he was still fast asleep. I took a deep breath and let it out slowly. Then just stood in the warm room and stared at the wizard. He lay on his side, his face pressed into the pillows. His eyebrows twitched like a dog dreaming, but the rest of his face was slack. His soft breaths shifted the blankets slightly, and I marveled at his ability to sleep so deeply. I hadn't been quiet stumbling out of the bed. His dark hair was mussed from sleep, sticking to his head in some places and straight out in others. It was adorable, really.

After a few moments, I finished examining his features and crossed to the door, hoping the inn had a bathing room. I was sticky and gross from the day's travel, and the night dressed too warmly.

After trying every door on the floor and finding them all locked, I returned to the small room where Merlin still slept and curled up on the edge of the bed, leaving a gap between the wizard and myself. I let my mind wander back to the past, picking up where I had left off the night before.

CHAPTER FIFTEEN

Ten years earlier.

Every evening for the next week I spent an hour in Merlin's cottage, trying different spells which he taught me. It came easily. Too easily.

He would show me something, like his magic ball of sparks, and I would copy him exactly, always uttering the same words. "I am not worthy."

Merlin would flinch when I uttered them but never said anything about the words that came naturally to me until one evening when I finally confronted him.

"Why don't you use the same words I do to form magic?" I asked. "I can't seem to do anything without them."

Merlin sighed and sat down at his kitchen table. "There is a legend behind that necklace you wear." He rubbed his clean-shaven jaw. "Minerva was said to be the goddess of many things, including wisdom and warfare.

The owl is considered to be her animal and is the source of her power."

I gripped the necklace which hung at my neck. "It's this Minerva's magic that I'm using?"

He nodded, then ran his fingers through his hair before rising. "Now, let's get back to work, shall we?"

"Then who's magic do you use?" I asked.

Merlin sighed. "You are an inquisitive thing, aren't you?"

His words brought an image forward in my mind of a great battle. I was much older, and it appeared Merlin and I were fighting. My magic was all hot flames and radiated anger, while his magic was cool like water and wanted to soothe me. It raged on though. Our magics clashing in an unending battle that shattered the world around us. Destroying everything in our wake.

I shook back to the moment and realized that Merlin was staring at me with a concerned expression. "Where did you go?"

"What?" I asked, unsure I wanted to explain what I had seen. It was a figment of my imagination, I was sure. Some strange waking dream.

"Did you see something?" he pressed.

"No. Tell me about your magic."

He stared at me for a long moment, but a knock at the door stole his attention. "My magic is a long story, one I will tell you someday, but not today." He rose and turned the lock on the cottage door, admitting Jag and Lady Ethel along with the little boy they had adopted from the orphanage.

Lady Ethel offered me a wide grin. "You are looking well, Morgana."

"Thank you, so are you," I replied. She did look well. She radiated from her place on the soldier's arm, with the toddler on her other hip. Their family was beautiful and made me miss mine all the more. It came in waves, these days. I had enough good people in my life, to balance out the bad, but I still missed my mother and sisters in the moments of quiet time, or when I saw a happy family like the one before me.

"I just came to give you some news, Merlin, but I suppose it will affect Morgana, too," Jag sat down at the kitchen table across from me. His kind eyes looked almost sad, and my heart began to race in my chest. "We have our marching orders and the commander has us leaving first thing in the morning for the west coast."

"What?" I gasped rising from my seat.

"I'm sorry, Morgana, I know you have made friends among the soldiers, but a new commander will be taking over the station. I'm sure Commander Artorius will ensure you keep your job."

"What about Copper?" tears welled in my eyes. I was losing too much, too quickly. The stables had become my home because of the people there... and the foal.

"Yes, the commander will ensure you can keep Copper at the stables until you come of age and find a new home or marry."

Those were the most dreadful of words. I would never marry. Not after meeting my stepfather and spending a year watching him destroy my family and the life I had loved. But I would find a home for myself someday, and as long as I could keep my horse, I wouldn't lose everything again.

Tears ran freely down my face and I wanted to jump into the soldier's arms, but Commander had told me I must be strong, so I wiped my tears and said my goodbyes. Hugging Lady Ethel and the little boy she had chosen from among us all. I told myself not to be jealous of the little boy; he deserved happiness as much as any of us. I calmly said goodnight to Merlin and left.

It wasn't until I was across the road that I broke into a run, heading not for my bed, but for the stable and the man who had given me hope for a life in what was one of my darkest days.

My boots slapped the packed ground as I raced through the city. I was used to running around the city, but this was different. My eyes clouded with new tears and I ran blindly, not caring if I were run over by a horse or carriage. I just needed to get back to the stables as fast as I could.

I passed a couple, holding hands and walking in the late evening. Then ran through the market that was closing up for the night. Men and women were piling their wares into wagons and heading back to their small farms outside of the town, but I barely noticed. I didn't stop until I rounded the tall fence of the riding school and came skidding to a stop in front of the closed barn doors. I unlatched them and pulled open the door to find it dark and empty inside. The tack was cleaned and sitting outside each stall door, ready to be put on the next morning. Flags on tall poles stood by the door. It was really true. They were prepared to leave in the morning.

I crept through the quiet barn; all the horses were munching hay or sleeping in their clean straw beds. When I got to Copper's stall door, I slid the latch open silently and stepped through into his stall. His dam was eating her hay, but Copper was spread out on the stall floor, fast asleep. I got down on my hands and knees and crawled to him with a sniffle. His tail flicked, and he opened his eyes, but he didn't lift his head, a silent invitation to join him in his comfortable bed.

So, I did. I crawled right over and lay my head on his shoulder, curling around the tired foal. I cried into his fur, letting his warmth seep into my bones and the smell of horse and stable calm my sorrow. The new commander could be a terrible person, worse than Mistress Carlyle or my stepfather. A tiny nicker brought me back to the moment, and I wiped my tears. I sighed. "Thank you, Copper. I promise I'll always take care of you, no matter what."

A soft sleepy nicker was my answer, and I fell asleep there on the floor of the stable, curled around my horse.

Voices woke me the next morning, early; the men preparing to ride out. Copper had already risen and was nursing at his dam's side when I stretched and rose to say my final goodbyes to the Commander and men who had let me be a part of their world. I reminded myself to be grateful for what I had been given, not mourn what I was losing, but it didn't help.

"There you are!" Commander Artorius said when he caught sight of me. "Did you sleep in that stall?"

I reached up and plucked some straw out of my hair. "I wanted to be here to say goodbye," I said, stifling a sob.

"Oh, little girl. This is not goodbye. I'm sure we will meet again someday. Let's just say farewell."

I swallowed twice before I felt I could speak without sobbing. "Farewell, Commander Artorius."

"Farewell, Morgana, and when next we meet, you may call me Lucius. That's what my family calls me. Now, will you help me get Fargo saddled and ready?"

"Yes, sir."

I couldn't reach to saddle his horse, but the commander enjoyed watching his big mean stallion drop his head to my lap so I could put on his bridle. The horse had a bad temper, but from the moment we had met that fateful day he had never put a foot wrong in my presence, and today was no different.

His nose nearly rested at my feet as I slid the bit into his mouth and did up the buckles to ensure his bridle was fit perfectly. A few times my eyes clouded with tears again, but I forced them down, determined to stay strong.

Before the sun was even fully in the sky, the men mounted their horses and rode out of town, flags flying high. I waited until long after I could no longer hear their hooves, standing silently in the open door of the nearly empty stable.

My knees grew weak at the loneliness that filled the silence and threatened to give out, but a tiny nicker drew me back. Dragging me from the edge and forcing my legs to turn me around and face the future. I stared down the empty barn aisle to the very end where a whiskery nose peeked over the stall door, begging me to come and play.

After a deep steadying breath, I crossed the hollow barn to where Copper waited, then slid open the stall door and stepped inside. Copper's little toothless mouth grabbed onto my shirt and began gumming it while I stroked his soft coat.

We would be okay, Copper and me. Maybe even better than okay. The future was undecided.

CHAPTER SIXTEEN

I wasn't sure what Merlin had said or done to Mistress Carlyle, but she never said a word to me about being late every night, nor did she raise her voice or cane to me again.

In the week that the army stables were vacated, I found I had too much time on my hands and ended up at the orphanage most of the day.

Mistress Carlyle gave a list of chores each morning and we completed them all. Everything from scrubbing the walls and windows, to clearing out the attic to make room for more orphaned children. The youngest took over the girls' room and we older girls ended up in the dusky attic once all the old furniture and crates of moth-chewed linens were moved out.

"Where do you go in the evening?" Breena asked one afternoon while we were cleaning the floors in the attic.

"I have a tutor," I said, thinking it was the best reply. Merlin was tutoring me, but in magic, not reading or writing.

"How did you get a tutor?" Lily asked, brushing the hair out of her face with the back of her arm. Her hands were black from the dirt and soot that stained the floor.

"He is a distant relative, I think." I didn't want the girls to be jealous of me as I had only just started to consider them my friends. But I needed a plausible reason someone would help an orphan.

"Why doesn't he just adopt you then?" Breena sounded put out.

"He isn't married. I don't think he will be in Pons Aelius long." I wrung out my cloth again, but it was no use. The water in my pail was too dirty. Pushing to my feet, I picked up my bucket and turned to the steep stairs.

"Morgana, can you take my bucket, too?" Breena asked. I was glad she wasn't angry with me. So, I turned back and took her bucket before teetering down the narrow treads to the second floor. Our old bedroom was packed full of small beds; each contained a toddler that had been laid down for a nap. I couldn't imagine that the orphanage could handle any more children, but I knew that Mistress Carlyle had plans to take in more, perhaps many more. When I asked her how we would handle more children, she simply said it was necessary and to mind my business. So, that's what I did.

Outside I dumped the dirty water into the grass and walked north to the River Tyne. It wasn't far from the orphanage, and Mistress Carlyle insisted the exercise was good for us. The sun shone bright and warm on my shoulders, but the trees were changing colours as autumn replaced summer. The last few days had delivered the heavy rains that always proceeded the winter, so I knew this sunny day was one of the few left.

At the water's edge, I squatted and filled both pails, then stood and turned to go back, but the group of boys, led by Eli, blocked my way, having somehow snuck up on me.

"What do you want?" I asked Eli since I knew he was the leader of the group of dirty boys.

"You shouldn't be here."

I lifted the pails. "It's where we get water to clean." His statement was stupid, so I replied in the most basic of terms.

His eyes narrowed and his fists balled, but he didn't step closer. I knew he was afraid of me from the way he had been avoiding me, even at mealtimes, he would pretend I didn't exist.

"I mean in this city, living under the same roof as us. In the southern cities, they hang sorceresses. Maybe we should start doing that here." His eyes bored into me. I had a few magic spells, but nothing that would stop the boy from handing out his death sentence, if he so chose. The boys outnumbered and surrounding me.

"Get out of my way, or I'll light you all on fire." I took a bold step forward and a few of the boys took a step back, including Eli. But his face contorted into a rage, his cheeks flushing as he stepped forward again to tower over me.

My bluff hadn't worked. I could make a ball of fire, but it wouldn't burn, and Merlin had told me not to use magic in public. There was no place more public than along the shore, though it was just me and the boys at the moment.

Hesitating for a moment longer, Eli observed me like I was a stray cat he wanted to mess with, but wasn't sure if I would use my claws. Then in a movement so fast I barely saw it coming, his hand lashed out, punching me in the side of the head.

I slammed to the ground, dropping the buckets and splashing water all over myself. The world swam as my vision faded in and out. Eli's fingers tangled in my long hair and he dragged me to my feet, though I couldn't stand.

"Come on, boys. We have a witch to hang." Eli laughed, the sound coming out like a goose honking as he dragged me along behind him. The other boys cheered and followed. I still couldn't see straight, but when they pulled me into a dark alley between a few buildings, a panic started deep in my stomach. That panic shot sparks in front of my eyes as my arms and legs began to flail, a useless effort to free myself.

A sudden image of myself came to my mind. I was an adult, standing in the middle of a city, my arms raised with a vicious look on my face. A snarl that curled the corners of my mouth. The city around me shook and rubble began to fall from the stone buildings. I didn't recognize the city but could hear the screams of the people as they ran into the street. I pulled on some inner part of myself and flashes of lightning dropped from the sky at my command, striking every living human and casting them to the ground.

My voice seemed hollow when the image of myself in the vision laughed and cackled at the puny humans.

I snapped back to my surroundings, just as Eli slid a rope over my head and tightened it around my neck. A hard pair of hands grabbed my wrists and held them behind my back.

The coarse material of the rope bit into my skin and bile rose in my throat. I swallowed it down and screamed at the top of my lungs. The boy who was holding my arms, slid one hand over my mouth and I bit down on the flesh. Hot blood poured into my mouth as he screamed and let me go. A fist slammed into my stomach, knocking all the air from my lungs. Panic rose higher as the rope around my throat pulled up. I turned my face to the sky and saw the rope was slung over a metal pole that hung between the two buildings. My hands went to my throat, and I began pulling at the rope, but my weight prevented it from loosening.

I looked down and watched as the boys leaned back into the rope, lifting my feet off the ground. Eli sneered and growled as he pulled. His face contorted like that of a demon. My fear overwhelmed me.

I couldn't speak or scream, with my windpipe cut off by the vicious tightening of the rope, but I flailed my legs and swung as my fingernails dug at my neck.

My vision began to fade as greyness took over. My panic fading to a pleasing calmness as my body went numb and my mind slowly closed down. Just as my sight was turning black, something rose from deep in my stomach like a flickering spark. It burned hard and deep as if I was suddenly on fire. My hands dropped from my neck as the new pain fought to overpower the old.

My vision returned and my hands seemed to lift of their own will until both were pointed straight at Eli. His frown turned to one of shock as my eyes bore into his.

I mouthed the word "die" and he collapsed to his knees, then fell right on his face. The rest of the boys weren't strong enough to hold me off the ground, and I crashed to the dirt. The rope loosened and I gasped for breath, falling to my side, near enough to Eli to see his lifeless eyes staring blankly ahead.

One of the other boys nudged Eli, bending down to look at him. "He's dead!" the boy shouted. His enthusiasm to kill me vanished and his concern for himself, something he should have had sooner, reared its head as his eyes turned towards me.

I lifted my hand to point at him and he screamed, turning and racing out of the alley, passing the remaining boys whose self-preservation instinct was a bit slower. My eyes turned to them as I fought to my knees, tearing the rope from my neck. I lifted my hand again and the rest of the boys wisely took off, leaving me alone in the alley with the dead body of my tormentor.

My lungs burned as I gasped for air until my heart settled. My neck throbbed with the stinging burn of the rope and my own nails which I could tell had gouged long streaks of blood into my skin.

Once I caught my breath again, I rose on shaking legs and left the alley. I didn't care about the stupid boy; he could rot there, for all I cared.

I returned to the river which was now occupied by a few women washing clothes, but I paid them no attention. Instead, I knelt in the mud on the shore, cupped the cool water and splashed it on my tear-stained face and burning neck. I hadn't even realized I was crying until my body shook like the earth under a thousand hooves. I dropped my head into my hands and let the tears fall. Magic may have saved me, but it also brought this pain.

I thought back to the heat in my stomach. The ease at which I had killed Eli. I had killed him. I felt the flame flicker inside me as if it were ready to repeat the same action and I felt the guilt. The sudden pain of knowing I had killed a person. He may have been trying to kill me, but I had killed him as easily as breathing.

I rose to my feet and ran. I had to find Merlin. He would know what to do.

The city blurred past as I ran. The people and carriages and men on horseback seemed distant, but my feet continued to hit the ground in a steady rhythm until the tiny cottage came into view. It was the only thing that seemed clear in the world gone sideways. The comfy cottage looked like home.

I skidded to a stop at the door, my hand already knocking on the door as I huddled against the wooden slats. I kept knocking, frantic, until the door swung open and I stumbled in.

"Whoa," Merlin's strong arms caught me and gathered me up. My body relaxed, conforming to his as he scooped up my small frame. My mother or father hadn't carried me in years, and my stepfather never carried me, but Merlin's arms circled me, making me feel safe and protected.

New sobs started. I hadn't been aware the last time I nearly died, but this time I had not only been aware but had killed the boy who was trying to kill me. I had fought back and won.

Merlin stroked my hair back and his eyes fell on the bruising and scratches at my neck.

"I'm sorry," I rasped, my voice harsh, barely above a whisper.

"What have you done?" he asked, his voice no louder than mine.

CHAPTER SEVENTEEN

Merlin let me lay in his arms as the shaking and crying subsided, and then long after I had stopped, still he held me. My hands were tucked in tight to my chest.

"Heal yourself. I can't stand to look at you like this. Please, Morgana."

His voice was pleading and sad, shaking me out of my own sorrow. Instead of the soft words of my mother scrolling across my mind, the tiny flame in my stomach burned to life. I felt it flickering like a moth on a lamp. Tiny sparks spit and grew until it felt like the fire might overwhelm me. I reached my hand up to touch my neck and felt the warmth jump through my fingers and into the damaged flesh on my neck.

"Heal," I said, my lips forming the word before I could think about it. The skin tingled, and the pain faded.

Finally, I cleared my throat and my eyes rose to meet Merlin's.

He had a shocked expression on his face and his body was tense, though he still held me.

I pushed away from him. Afraid by the look on his face that he would reject me. I knew in my gut it wasn't the same magic that I had been using, that he had been teaching me to control and use.

"I'm sorry," I whispered again, turning and heading for the door. My heart couldn't stand to watch him reject me. I would rather leave and never return.

"Morgana, wait."

I stopped at the door but didn't turn around.

"Tell me." His voice was soft and tender. Not the disappointment or anger I had been expecting.

I slowly turned to face him, leaning back against the door frame and twirling one of my long red curls around my finger nervously.

"A boy tried to hang me. I did something bad to him. I'm sorry." My voice was still small and barely above a whisper.

"What boy? The same who hurt you before?"

I nodded, dropping my eyes to the ground.

"What did you do?"

I licked my lips and shifted on my feet. "Killed him."

Merlin rose and took long steps towards me, stopping right in front of me, nearly toe to toe. I felt small and helpless there. I had used my magic in public and I deserved whatever punishment Merlin decided on, but my heart broke at the thought. The previous weeks I had spent working hard to impress him with my control and ability to learn.

Merlin crouched down in front of me, so we were eye to eye.

His hands rose slowly as if I were a wild animal and he feared to scare me away. It wasn't the reaction I was expecting, but when his hands stopped and gripped my upper arms, pulling me towards him, I sagged into his arms.

"You did the right thing. You are too important to be ruined by a foolish boy. We have much to do."

The memory of the vision of myself destroying the city came flooding back. I opened my mouth to tell him, but the moment was too good. Having someone who cared about me felt like a relief and I didn't want to ruin it. But if I didn't tell him, would I really grow to ruin whole cities? I had too much power, and I knew it. What if I felt threatened and reacted without thinking? I was out of control.

I let Merlin hold me a moment longer, then pushed away and opened my mouth to tell him what I had seen, but a knock at the door stopped my words.

Merlin grinned at me. "Why don't you go have a snack at the table."

I grinned and nodded, then walked past him to the table as he opened the door and the sound of men's voices murmured across the cottage.

On the table was a block of cheese and a loaf of bread, still warm. My mouth watered. I hadn't eaten yet since Lady Ethel left and no longer brought me sandwiches at the stables and Mistress Carlyle didn't believe children should eat in the morning. The knife slid through the block of cheese, cutting a piece, then I poured a glass of water from the pitcher on Merlin's table and tore a piece of bread off. I wished, not for the first time, that he would adopt me and let me live with him.

I brought the bread and cheese to my mouth, but a new vision invaded my mind. The sight of Merlin and I standing on the deck of a boat. The ocean spread out around us as far as I could see. Merlin's arm was over my shoulders. I stood nearly as tall as him, fully grown and wearing a long green dress. Merlin's mouth was moving, but I couldn't hear the words he used. I smiled at him and felt a pleasant feeling in my stomach at the twinkle of his blue eyes.

I looked at him the way my mother used to look at my father and knew instinctively that Merlin would never adopt me, but fate would link us somehow when I was grown.

My mind snapped back to the present at the sound of the door closing. Merlin turned to me, a look of almost sadness etched his face, but when he caught my eye, his usual smile tugged the corners of his mouth up. He smoothed out his shirt and stepped into the small kitchen, taking a seat across from me.

His large hands took up the knife and sliced himself some bread and cheese, then poured a cup of water, his place setting matching mine.

He grinned at me and we ate in silence. I wasn't sure why he had looked so unhappy when he returned from speaking to whoever was at the door, but it seemed forgotten now.

"I should go back to the orphanage and help clean the floors. Mistress Carlyle will be unhappy if I'm gone too long."

Merlin grunted but didn't stop me when I rose to my feet, carrying my plate to the counter where he had a small pan of water for washing.

"Thank you," I said.

"Don't thank me. It's the least I can do."

His words made no sense to me, but I let them go as I crossed to the door.

"Morgana, come back tonight so we can talk about your magic."

I turned to look at him, but he wasn't looking at me, his gaze was intent on the cup of water in his hand.

"Okay," I replied before slipping out the door. Worry gathered in my stomach, making the bread and cheese feel like a heavyweight, but I swallowed down my feelings and forced my legs to pick up a run. I had to get myself back to the orphanage and come up with a good reason for having lost the buckets.

CHAPTER EIGHTEEN

Present.

"What the hell kind of magic was that?" I burst out, startling Merlin out of his breakfast. Others in the small dining room of the inn stared at me, but I apologized quietly, and they went back to their breakfasts.

"What are you referring to?" Merlin asked.

"The magic I used to kill that boy," I whispered. "It was some kind of fire in my stomach."

Merlin looked away, his teeth worrying on his bottom lip as if he were a nervous schoolboy. It would have been endearing if I wasn't so upset. I hadn't used a dark arts word, but I had killed that boy anyway. I could feel a warmth in my stomach as if the magic from my memory was stirring to life.

"Merlin," I said, reaching out and taking his hand with mine. His palm was soft and warm, and I paused, flushing at the feeling as his hand turned and his fingers twined with mine.

My eyes shifted from our hands to his eyes, and I found he was watching me with a serious and intent look. I tried to tug my hand away, but he held on and I felt the warmth of his hand grow until it was hot. It ignited the fire that sparked in my stomach as if his magic was pulling mine forward. This foreign magic grew and leaped about, racing up my arm and down to my fingers to slip past my fingertips and mingle with Merlin's. I felt a deep connection to him; the familiarity growing into something more.

His eyes shifted from blue to green then back to a dark blue as deep as the sea. It enraptured me. I couldn't look away, and I didn't want to.

"Why was this gone for so long?" The spark curled and leaped as if it was happy to reclaim its place within me.

"Keep going, Morgana." Merlin's voice was thick with an emotion I didn't recognize. "We will stay here until you have it all back. I can't risk taking you across the sea without your memories in place."

I nodded and he let my fingers slip out of his. He returned to the last of his meal.

I tried to finish eating, but instead, I let my memories flood back in. Like a high tide, they swept me away.

CHAPTER NINETEEN

Ten years earlier.

That night I returned to Merlin's cottage, but he wasn't home. I knocked and waited over an hour, but he didn't come home or didn't answer his door, anyway.

I walked back to the orphanage, disappointed and worried. Perhaps Merlin had left the city without saying goodbye. The new commander and his army were meant to move into the stables in the morning, so I knew I needed to get to sleep early and be up at the crack of dawn to set up the stalls, but instead, I wandered the streets and considered what could have happened to Merlin. I passed his house a few more times, each time knocking and listening intently for any movement inside, but when I heard nothing, I moved on.

My legs grew tired as the moon rose high in the night sky and finally, I dragged myself back to the orphanage and crept up the stairs to the attic where the other girls were already fast asleep.

I kicked off my boots and lay back in my lumpy bed. Just as I was falling asleep, the vision I had seen of myself destroying a city came flooding back in and I couldn't stop it. The screams of the people being crushed rang through the silent room, and I covered my ears, closing my eyes tight. But it wasn't real, so the sound still echoed, and the sights still chilled me to the bone. Lightning crashed to the earth, hitting close to where I stood, but I held my ground as if the lightning was mine to control.

I opened my mouth to scream at it to stop, but a firm hand slid over my mouth. Shocked I opened my eyes to find Merlin standing over me. I was in the attic still. He shouldn't have been there.

When I calmed, he took his hand away, and I whispered, "What are you doing here?"

He straightened and curled his finger to indicate I should follow him, then walked silently to the door. I threw off the blanket and yanked on my boots, chasing him out of the room and down the stairs.

I followed all the way to the yard where he stood in the darkness, his head hanging as if he was inspecting his shoes, but as I approached, I realized his eyes were closed.

"What did you see?" he asked, without looking up.

"What?" I asked.

"I know you are having visions, Morgana. Tell me what it was you saw."

I bit my lip and stalled for time. "How do you know that I had a vision? It could have just been a nightmare."

Merlin finally looked up at me, one eyebrow raised as if I had asked a foolish question. I knew that look by now.

My boot scuffed on the ground, but I couldn't think of any way out of it, so I told him about the vision. About my face and the people dying and the havoc I had caused.

Merlin's face went paler and paler as I explained the scene to him. When I finished, he just stood and stared at me. He shook his head, then bit his lip.

"It's not really a vision, is it? Couldn't it just be my imagination?" I asked, wishing I could snatch my words out of the air so he would never have to make that sad and worried expression.

"It's a vision. Of the future. Your future."

My knees gave out, and I collapsed to the cool damp dirt. My body felt numb. How could I do that to so many innocent people? It wasn't possible.

I looked up at Merlin, his face was still white, but he looked down at me. "It's fine. We can fix this."

"How can we fix it? If it's a vision, it's the future, right?"

"No," he said. "It's a possible future. We just have to change it. We can take away your magic."

All the air left my lungs. I had just begun to use magic. My ability was natural, and magic came easily to me, but if it would cause destruction beyond my imagination, I would gladly give it up. What use was magic, if I couldn't use it, anyway? I had to hide it from everyone. The few boys who knew about it hadn't so much as glanced in my direction since the incident in the alley. They proved to have more intelligence than Eli had.

"Do it," I said.

Merlin shook his head. "It won't be that easy. You will have to help. We will have to work together to make the spell that will strip your magic and your memory of it. Including your memory of me."

"What? No way. I can't just forget you. I need you. You are my only friend."

Merlin's face crumpled. "I would give you anything. But I can't give you this, Morgana. You must trust that this will be for the best and your future will be better."

I shook my head and tears tipped over my eyelids to streak hot down my cheeks. "You can't go!"

"I have to go, anyway. I'm needed elsewhere, but we will meet again when the time is right. For now, go back to your bed and sleep. I need a few days to get things organized, but I'll come for you when I'm ready to do the spell."

His arms wrapped around me and I got lost in the protection he offered. My heart was still racing at the thought of never knowing him. I could live without magic, but how would I live without Merlin? I thought of the Commander and the army men who had left, too, and when Merlin set me on my feet, I felt like a boat set adrift, the gap between us growing larger and wider until I could barely see him.

"I'm sorry it has to be this way, but it's temporary."

"Everything is temporary," I replied. "That excuses nothing."

Merlin swallowed harshly and laughed once without humour, but then he turned and strode away.

My emotions went numb to match my body, and I returned to my bed but didn't sleep that night. I stayed awake and watched the moon on its trip through the sky. When the sun finally kissed the horizon, I rose and pulled my boots back on before heading down to the stables.

It was a new day and the new commander with his army would arrive in a few hours. I threw down hay, scrubbed water buckets and filled them, ensuring each stall was perfectly clean and well-bedded for the incoming horses. I spent some time working on Copper's leading skills. He was improving, but my heart wasn't really in it. He noticed and was acting up. His teeth found my flesh more than once, leaving round bruises behind.

I gave up on training and went back to cleaning. No cobwebs were safe from my broom as I cleared the stables with the door wide open to get the dust out. I found an old rag and scrubbed the front of each stall until the old worn wood gleamed. Just as I finished the last one, I heard the sound of many hooves pounding on the packed earth.

I grabbed the bucket of dirty water and dumped it out the back door before putting it away in the feed room and returning to the aisle to meet the new commander and his army.

The men were large and bushy, similar to Commander Artorius' men, but were serious as they led their horses through and into stalls. They stripped their tack off and rubbed down their horses with practiced, calculated movements. Once all the horses were seen to, and the tack hung outside the stalls, the men stood at attention, waiting for inspection. The commander was the last to finished with his horse but seemed in no hurry as he sauntered down the aisle, inspecting each man and horse as he went.

When he reached the end, he turned on his heel and his eyes fell on me. He narrowed his eyes, inspecting me like I was an ant under his boot. He stopped in front of me and glared down at me.

"You must be the girl that Artorius mentioned. He said you do chores here in exchange for coins and the keep of a colt he granted you."

The commander continued his inspection of me. As he hadn't asked a question, I didn't reply, but I studied him from beneath my eyelashes. He was tall and imposing, his beard so thick I couldn't see his mouth. It had streaks of grey in it that matched his hair. His uniform was immaculate, the colours bold and saturated like none I had ever seen before. A chain of gold swept from his vest button to his pocket and gold-colored accents marked his chest and shoulders and the hat he held in one hand.

"Are you strong, girl?" he asked after a moment of tense silence.

"Yes, sir," I replied. I was strong for a child my size, but my magic was stronger than anything Merlin had seen. Too strong, I thought.

"Hmm." The commander's thick hand rose to scratch at his beard, making an unpleasant sound in the silence broken only by the chewing of the horses in their stalls. "Very well, then. I'll give you a chance, but if you fail in your duties, I won't keep you. Also, my men clean their own stalls, so I will only need you for half days from now on. You are dismissed."

My eyes shot up to him in shock. I wasn't prepared to spend another half day at the orphanage. I would much rather clean stalls than scrub floors, but the commander turned away from me, so I hurried out the door.

Once I was away from the stables, I stopped and leaned against the front of a wooden house. I should have been glad that I still had a job half the day, but I mourned the loss, anyway.

Slowly, I made my way back to the orphanage, determined to make the best of it.

When I arrived back home, the boys were outside chopping more wood. The younger ones were gathering branches as kindling and stacking them beside the larger logs. The boys who knew about me didn't look my way; they kept their eyes carefully turned to their work.

Inside the girls were scrubbing the kitchen floor.

"Hey, Morgana. You here to help?"

I grinned at Lilly and Breena who were on their knees, their clothes dirty and wet. "Yup. I'll be around more now. The new commander only wants me there for the morning."

"Humph."

We all turned to find Mistress Carlyle in the doorway. Her dark eyes inspecting me. "Does that mean you'll only bring in half the pay?"

I hadn't wanted to tell her, hoping I could spend a bit of time watching the men ride each day, but now that she knew, I was out of luck.

"I don't know, ma'am," I replied, grabbing a rag and joining the girls on the floor.

"Then you will be responsible for half a day's chores here as well. I expect you home promptly at noon."

"Yes ma'am," I replied, dunking the rag in the dingy water and slopping it onto the wood floor.

She walked away, and I got down to work.

By the time we were done, there was a knock at the front door of the House, and I heard Mistress Carlyle open it and the low murmuring of voices. "Morgana," Mistress Carlyle said. "Someone is here for you."

I rose, my knees dirty and wiped my wet hands on my skirt before turning to find Merlin and an older woman with a cane standing in the parlour.

The woman with the cane was the opposite of Merlin. She was shorter than Mistress Carlyle and had a pleasant look on her face. Her clothes were basic and made of sturdy material. She wore a broad-brimmed hat and sweater that were appropriate for the changing seasons, but not lavish or fancy in any way.

"Hello," I said.

The woman grinned at me. "Hello, Morgana. My name is Miss Landers."

CHAPTER TWENTY

Present

"Whoa!" I shouted, scaring Merlin again. We were sitting in the room Merlin had rented for us. He had been reading, but the book now lay face down on his lap and his hand clutched his chest.

"Morgana, I wish you would stop doing that."

"I'm sorry. I just didn't realize I had known Miss Landers before. Why didn't she say anything?" I thought back to every moment I had alone with the older woman who had housed me on Avalon. She had a million opportunities to tell me that I had met her before but hadn't.

"We agreed not to. Not unless you were a danger to yourself or others."

I let that thought sink in. "You think I'm a danger?" I laughed as soon as the words were out of my mouth. I had killed a bunch of people. I was a murderer.

My laughter died as the realization of what I had done truly sunk in. Innocent people had died, and I was responsible.

"Oh no," Merlin whispered as he watched my face change from humour to horror, and on to deep sadness. "Please don't cry." His voice was pleading, but I couldn't stop the sobs that began to wrack my body. I tried to crumple into a heap, but strong arms swept me up until I found myself wrapped up with my face pressed into Merlin's chest. His scent of wood fire and horse sweat. It was comforting to be in his arms. As if his strength gave me strength. His warm hand rubbed up and down my back, calming my frazzled nerves.

"I'm so foolish," I whispered when the sobs subsided.

"You aren't foolish. You have always fought to stay alive. That is a very good character trait as far as I can tell."

I looked up at Merlin, his stubbly beard framing his square jaw and his eyes offering a serious expression I had rarely seen on him. I wanted to take all my words and tears back so he would return to the twinkling eyes and curled lips of his usual expression. Instead, I made it worse.

"I wasn't in real danger in Avalon. They would have taken me back to Rome. I could have escaped at any other time, but instead, I killed everyone in that building. Children."

Merlin sighed. "We can't undo that, but you can learn and move forward. There is good you can do, Morgana."

I scoffed and rested my head back on Merlin's chest, unwilling to give up the comfort even if I didn't deserve it. "What good could I possibly do?"

"There is a whole big world out there that needs help. People starving because of crops withering, disease spreading faster than anyone can escape, an evil that lurks in the shadows."

I thought about that for a moment as Merlin's chest rose and fell in a slow steady motion that felt almost like the rocking of the fisherman's boat as he sailed me across to Avalon. If I could do great evil, I could do great good as well. The country was in ruins, thanks to the savages who plundered the shores. Rome was struggling to protect us from the Saxons when they were already fighting at home.

I let my eyes slide closed and imagined myself as a great queen, ruling over the country and ensuring the people had enough to eat and were safe from the invaders. It was so clear, I almost thought it was a vision, but it vanished as soon as I opened my eyes. I could return the law to the country. Ensure children had food to eat.

I let the thought linger in my mind for a while, then slid away from the present and back into the memories that were flowing so easily now.

CHAPTER TWENTY-ONE

Ten years earlier

Merlin and Miss Landers walked me back to Merlin's cottage in silence. I wanted to ask a million questions, but the silence was pleasant, and I knew the sooner I had my questions answered, the sooner I would lose Merlin and my memories of him.

When we finally turned the last corner, and the cottage came into view, I reached out and grabbed Merlin's hand. "Can't you just take me away from here? I promise I'll be good."

Merlin looked down at me with a sad and resigned expression. "I'm sorry, Morgana. It has to be this way for now. But I promise I'll come to find you someday."

CHAPTER TWENTY-TWO

Present.

"Wait! You said you wouldn't tell me about my past unless I was a danger to myself or others. But you promised to come to find me again. Was that a lie? Would you have left me alone my whole life if I hadn't killed those people?"

Merlin sighed. "I never wanted to leave you. I would have returned years ago, but when I checked upon you, you were fine and growing."

"You checked up on me?"

Merlin smoothed out my hair, his hand stopping to hold my head to his chest with gentle fingers. "Every time I passed Pons Aelius, which was often. I watched you grow from afar until you left. I was on my way to help you at Avalon when I heard the news and went in search of you." He grinned, but it was a sad expression. "I thought I would just help you with your writing."

"Miss Landers said someone was coming."

"Yes, I just wish I had arrived sooner to keep you from the fate that befell you. If anyone was foolish, it was me for thinking magic wouldn't find a way to you."

Silence fell upon us again, so I let the memories creep back in.

CHAPTER TWENTY-THREE

Ten years earlier.

Inside Merlin's cottage, we sat around his table and discussed what would be best to erase and what we could leave.

"I need Copper," I said. "If I'm losing everything else, I need my horse.

"Very well, we will keep Copper, but we have to remove Jag, so the entire army has to go. So does Lady Ethel," Merlin said. He had a point. They knew about my magic and had spoken to me about it.

"Then you are taking away everyone who was ever nice to me," I complained

"We can remove Eli, too. In fact, that was when you had the vision, so he definitely has to go."

I wouldn't miss that memory.

"Morgana," Miss Landers said. "We will need your help to do this spell."

"Yes," Merlin interrupted. "You must want to forget, or it won't work."

"I'll never want to forget you," I cried. "How can you ask that of me?"

"Because it's the only way, child," Miss Landers replied. "If you want a chance at a happy normal life without the darkness inside you."

I couldn't believe this was happening. I had finally found people who cared about me and I would have to forget them all. This was a nightmare. I dropped my head to my hands and wished I was sleeping. I rubbed the tears from my eyes and looked up again to find Merlin and Miss Landers both watching me.

"Don't cry, child," Merlin whispered. "We will meet again."

I sniffled and wiped my nose. "Fine, let's get on with it then," I said, praying it wouldn't work but also coming to terms with the idea that I had to do this if I wanted to save myself the future pain of destroying an entire city.

Merlin and Miss Landers each took one of my hands in theirs, then they held hands as well, forming a circle. The warmth gathered in my stomach and I wished that Merlin had told me more about magic before I gave it up. It didn't really matter now as I wouldn't have it much longer. This was my last spell.

Merlin's hand grew warm in mine and I felt the sparks and lightning explode in my stomach and rush to meet him where our hands were linked. A moment later, Miss Landers' hand was warm, too, and it felt like our circle was a ring of fire.

The soft scent of lavender rose in the room from Miss Landers' direction and I knew instinctively that it was her magic. It was clean and wholesome, not like the sparks shooting off in my stomach. But Merlin's magic was like my own: Hot and powerful and unnatural.

"You must want it, too, Morgana," Miss Landers' voice rose above the crackling of the fire in the fireplace. The fire had grown as if in response to our flame.

"I do want it, too," I said out loud, letting the truth of that wash over me. I didn't want to kill people. I wanted to save them all.

The fire grew in my stomach and rose to my head, burning away memories I once held as treasure. The memory of Jag lifting me up to the loft. The memory of evenings by the fire with Merlin as he wove spells for me. The sour pain of Eli, his face contorted with rage, then with pain as I killed him.

All the memories screamed like wet kindling in a funeral pyre as they burned from my memory. The one memory that remained, one I could cling to, was the lopsided colt with crooked legs. But I hadn't fixed him, I had simply lifted him every day until his legs grew strong and he could stand and nurse on his own. I had saved him the way a normal person would have when the cruel commander of the army wanted to kill him. My mind filled in details I didn't remember, making stories complete and fiction, fact.

It all tumbled together until the world went black.

I woke the next day, confused, but late for the stables. So, I rose and rushed out of the house, creeping past the Mistress Carlyle so I could find my way to my horse before I needed to begin work for the day.

I raced through the city, tripping only once in the still-dark morning light. Pulling open the door to the stable, a gentle nicker greeted me, and I grinned at the pleasure of my only friend. My sweet colt Copper.

His soft whiskers tickled my nose, and I kissed his tiny lips, careful to be quick enough he couldn't nip me with his budding teeth. I had learned those nips hurt more than anything.

"Hello, sweet boy. It's just you and I today. You ready for an adventure?"

I slipped on his halter and took him to the riding school to work on his leading until the men of the army rose for the day and would expect me to feed and water the horses. This was the best part of my day. The time I got to spend with Copper. Later I would be scrubbing and cooking for the children of the orphanage, but for now, I had my moment of freedom to enjoy the happiest part of my day.

CHAPTER TWENTY-FOUR

Present

"Just like that. You removed everything good from my life. Is that all, or is there more I don't know about?" I felt betrayed. Even though I had done it all to myself in a foolish attempt to prevent a future I didn't want. One that was probably meant to be anyway, based on what happened at Avalon.

I had been a child and didn't know the lasting ramifications of what I was doing, Merlin was an adult and should have done better. When I thought of all the things I had done and how terrible it had been at the orphanage, I couldn't believe he had left me there. I had spent years hungry, exhausted, and barely hanging on. The only joy I had was in the hours I spent with Copper, those always too fleeting.

"I knew you would blame me for that. The fault is mine. I should have found another way, but I was needed elsewhere and had no time to come up with a better plan." Merlin's face was somber and everything inside me wanted to take my words back so I could see his twinkling eyes and impervious grin again, but I couldn't. The pain felt too new, like a fresh cut, not a decade-old scar.

I shook my head and slid down on the bed until I was lying flat, then rolled onto my side, facing away from him. I needed a few minutes to process the information.

Merlin was silent, but I could feel his eyes watching me. He sighed after a few minutes. "I guess we can go to the Isle of Man now. You ready to go?" He rose and tucked the book he was reading into the small pack he attached to his saddle, then pulled on his boots.

Without a word, I pulled on my boots, too, and rose, leaving him behind. I shuffled down the stairs and around the old inn to the small stable that housed our horses.

Both Sara and Copper nickered at me, twisting my gut a bit more. I gave Sara a pat on my way past but collapsed into Copper's side as soon as I slipped through his stall door. He stood firm and let me lean against him. What would have become of me if I hadn't had the beautiful chestnut horse? He was like a beacon in my life. The only constant. I had no idea what was ahead for us, but I would make sure to always have Copper and keep myself guarded. I couldn't afford to lose anyone else, even if it was just temporary.

Merlin was tacking up Sara, but I ignored it until her stall door swung open and the grey mare nickered as her hooves travelled away from us.

Copper returned her call, and I swung his door open so we could follow. It wasn't like I had anywhere else to go.

Outside, snow swirled down from above and Merlin was astride Sara, waiting for us. So, I grasped Copper's mane and swung up onto his back with the practiced ease that came with several years of riding the ginger gelding.

We didn't go far, though. After strolling through the street, we reached the water's edge. The air was ice cold, and the water lapped at the shore like a predator eating its prey. I shivered beneath the tiger skin still wrapped around me, but Copper was warm and comforting beneath me.

I glanced around at the large boats docked there. They were massive, meant to take men and horses across the sea, but I had heard stories of the sickness spreading through them like wildfire and shivered at the thought of weeks aboard a boat, but I had no idea how far the Isle of

Man was. I would ask Merlin, but I didn't feel much like talking to him, so I bit my lip and let my fingers run through Copper's mane, pulling out the tangles.

I wasn't paying attention, but when Copper started walking, I looked up to see Merlin riding Sara towards a large ship with two masts. The sails were tucked in against the masts, but I could imagine what it looked like out at sea, both sails catching the wind. The side was open, and a ramp led from the end of the pier to the side of the boat.

Sara didn't even slow her forward march as she climbed the ramp and ducked her head, Merlin laying down on her withers, disappearing into the darkness of the ship. Copper strode forward, but I felt him hesitate.

I leaned down and slicked his coat with my hand. "You're fine, don't let Sara think you're weak. I know you're made of steel."

He strode on as if he understood my words, ducking into the boat. The ramp peaked at the door and descended into the darkness. Inside was warm and damp. Once my eyes adjusted, I found it to be full of horses, men seeing to them by filling mangers and tying them securely to a rope that strung along the rows.

That was when I heard a booming voice that I would recognize anywhere… well, now that my memories had returned. I leaped from Copper's back, abandoning him to his own devices, then wove between the horses and men as I followed the sound.

"Get your things organized, this is a disgrace," Commander Artorius said.

"Commander!" I yelled, before throwing myself at the poor man.

His big arms caught me, though he was smaller than I remembered. Some men whistled and catcalled, but I didn't let go. "Back to work," he said, and the men left abruptly.

"I'm sorry, m'lady. Have we met?" The commander's face was flushed as he set me on my feet. His hair was all grey now and his body slouched, but his eyes were the same and his beard, through grey to match his hair, was thick.

"Morgana," I said in the way of introduction.

The recognition struck his eyes immediately. "Oh, dear child, you have grown!"

I grinned up at him, unable to find words for a long moment. We just stared at each other. "Copper is here," I said to break the silence.

He grinned behind his beard. "That's wonderful. He must be getting older like the rest of us."

My smile fell. I wondered if Copper would ever get older now that I had brought him back to life. I forced the smile back on my face. "You would never know it."

Merlin walked up at that moment. "Morgana, would you like to introduce me to your friend?" he asked, eyeing the much bigger man.

"Commander Artorius, this is Merlin. Merlin, Commander Artorius." I went back to gawking at the Commander. It seemed almost like yesterday I had seen him last; the memories were so new. I felt young standing in front of him, and as if I needed to impress upon him my strength and worth. I was a grown woman now, but that didn't change how I felt.

"Ah, you've married! Any young ones about, then?" Commander asked.

"Oh, no. We are just travelling together. I've not married, Commander."

Merlin gave me a sly look but shook the Commander's offered hand. "I'm sure I'll convince her to settle down, eventually."

His words came as a shock to me. I may have thought the wizard was handsome, but he hadn't made any intentions known.

The Commander's deep chuckle rang through the boat. "I'm sure you will. She will be a fine wife. You know, she was more efficient than most of these men." The Commander's voice rose at the end and he hooked his thumb over his shoulder. His voice sent the men scurrying about tending to the horses.

"Well, I should get Morgana settled," Merlin said, slinging his arm around my shoulders. "But I'm sure she will seek you out to reminisce. We are aboard for a few days."

"Very well. Perhaps I'll see you both in the dining room. And, Morgana, don't forget I told you to call me Lucius last we spoke. We are family."

A tear tried to well in my eye, but I swallowed it back and hugged him once more. "Thank you, Lucius."

Merlin nodded once, gathering my back under his arm and turned us away, leading me through the rows of horses. I had wanted to stay and ask him about Jag and his horse, Fargo, though I didn't see the big bay stallion in the line, so worried that something bad had happened to him.

"The ship has a dining room?" I asked, distracting myself.

Merlin chuckled. "Not really, but most people eat on the deck."

I bit my lip until we came upon the horses, both tied to the high line and eating happily at their hay. Copper was wearing a piece of rope tied up like a halter and I couldn't help but chuckle. "He looks silly tied like that."

"Well, he should have a halter at least."

Merlin's words were off the cuff, but the sting settled in my bones and I remembered Paxton's gift. I wished I had taken the halter with me, instead of leaving it in the blood-soaked tent. I gave Copper a stroke on his forehead and then followed Merlin through the boat and up two ladders to reach the top deck. The boat was still docked but men were pulling ropes that lifted the ramp, covering the doorway. Voices shouted from the land and from behind us where men were pulling more ropes, and the boat began to float away from the dock, slowly at first, but then a bit faster.

Slowly the boat turned until it was facing away from the shore, and the men and women back on land got smaller and smaller. The wind slapped my face and fingers like a million bee stings, and I huddled down in my tiger skin.

The steady rocking as we moved out to sea lulled me. I had never been on a ship that size, but it felt safe.

Much safer than the tiny boat I had taken across to Avalon.

"So, tell me about the Isle of Man," I said, breaking the silence.

Merlin turned to me and grinned, the comfortable look back in his eyes as if my outburst at the inn had never happened.

"The island is much more than it appears. To most, it looks like a barely inhabited island, but to those with magic, it has a thriving population with much more to see and do. Plus, it's safe for those like us. "Merlin's hand reached out and pushed a strand of my hair behind my ear. His fingers brushed my cheek, sending my heart into a faster rhythm.

I wanted to ask him if he meant what he said about convincing me to settle down. I had no plans to marry. My mother and stepfather had set such a poor example of a marriage that I knew I never wanted that. But I couldn't bring myself to ask Merlin. He was so much older than me and I felt foolish even considering the idea that he liked me.

Luckily, before the silence got awkward again, there was a giant whoosh sound causing us both to turn as the sails dropped open and the wind grabbed on, pulling the boat forward. I stumbled, but Merlin's arms wrapped around me, holding me up.

"Thank you," I said, feeling heat flush my face.

"Anytime," he whispered. The serious tone and the look on his face suggested the word meant more than I understood.

CHAPTER TWENTY-FIVE

Merlin showed me to the cabin we would sleep in while onboard. It was painfully small, barely wide enough for one person to sleep in, never mind two. When I tensed, looking through the door, Merlin smiled.

"I won't require much sleep, so you can use the bed, Morgana." His tone was half humorous and half chiding, like I was a child he was explaining something to. I wanted to hide my face, but instead, I stepped inside and sat at the end of the tiny bed. It seemed soft enough and there were plenty of blankets.

Merlin placed his bag on the floor beside my feet. "Would you like to have a rest? I just need to meet up with someone, but I could meet you back here in time for dinner."

I nodded. "That would be great."

"All right. If you like to read, you are welcome to the book in my bag."

"Thanks," I said.

His eyes twinkled again as he watched me for a moment, then he turned back, stepping out of the small room. "I'll be back by dinner," he said in parting, then I was alone.

I rose and turned the lock on the door before I flopped back on the bed. "What is wrong with me?" I asked the splotched ceiling. I tucked my fingers under my back, trying to warm them. It would have been nice to start a small fire, but it was too risky with so many people around and only the flimsy lock to keep them out. I pulled the blanket over myself and curled beneath it, shivering hard a few times until the blanket warmed with my heat and my muscles relaxed.

I thought of Copper and hoped he was being good and staying calm, but it was only a few moments before my eyes drifted closed and I fell into sleep.

A knocking on the door woke me. "Morgana, open up!" In my groggy state, I almost didn't recognize Merlin's voice, but when he repeated himself, I threw back the covers and rose, unlocking the door. He pushed the door open so fast I fell back on the bed. Merlin slipped in and shut the door behind him, quickly locking it again.

"What's going on?" I asked.

Merlin's clothes were all disheveled and his hair was messy. He was also breathing hard as if he had been running around the ship.

"What is wrong with you?" I asked.

He finally turned and looked at me, pushing his hair off his forehead, then biting his lip like he was trying not to tell me.

I raised my eyebrows at him, but when he still didn't speak, I flopped back on the bed. "Fine, whatever. More secrets."

Merlin sighed heavily before the foot of the bed sagged as he crumpled down. "Please don't hate me forever. I wouldn't have done that to you if I had thought of another way to change the future. You have to believe me."

"I don't hate you. I just don't like secrets and lies."

Merlin sighed. "There is a man on the ship who is determined to remove my head from my body. He knows I have magic and thinks I turned his wife against him."

I sat up and looked at him. "Did you?"

"No. Not really. I mean I might have told her something he did when we were young and foolish." His mischievous grin told me there was no 'might have' about that. "But how was I to know that she would take it so seriously?"

That just opened up a whole new set of questions. "What did you do?"

Merlin glanced back at me. "Nothing."

I laughed at his red cheeks. Oh, he did something. "Well, whatever. So, you will have to stay in here until we get to the Isle of Man."

Merlin sighed again. "There isn't space for two in here. At least not comfortably."

"Then we will be uncomfortable," I replied, scooting over as close to the wall as I could.

Merlin occupied more space than I expected, and we were basically pressed together. "I'm sorry."

"It's fine. Tell me a story," I said almost out of habit. He used to tell me stories when I was young when he wanted to teach me a lesson about some type of magic of another.

"Very well, I will fill you in on the details of your mother's magic." He settled back on the bed. Our faces were still very close together.

"Minerva is the goddess of wisdom and warfare, as I told you before, but the story of her origin is long and confusing. But it mostly revolves around Metis, the mother of wisdom, and Jupiter, the god of sky and thunder. Jupiter knew the prophecy was that his own son would overthrow his rule of the heavens as he had done to Saturn."

"Fearing that their child would be male, Jupiter swallowed Metis whole after tricking her into turning herself into a fly. Metis continued to live inside Jupiter as his wisdom. Some others say Metis was simply a vessel for the birth of Minerva."

"Either way, the constant pounding, and ringing in Jupiter's head left him in agonizing pain. To relieve that, Vulcan, the god of fire and volcanoes, used a hammer to split Jupiter's head and from the cleft emerged Minerva, as an adult in full battle armour."

I thought about the tale for a long moment. As the silence stretched, Merlin's grin came back to his face. "That is a ridiculous story," I said, shaking my head.

"Well, that is how the story goes. Whether it is a good tale or not, it is a story, of sorts."

I shook my head. "Can we work on magic in here?" I had a lot of catching up to do. Magic of various types pulled at me to use it. Mainly the Dark Arts, which I had used little since the incident in Avalon.

"Small things should be fine. Don't do too much."

I held out my hand between us and said "Byrne." The flame flickered to life, a tiny light that made Merlin's face glow.

"You shouldn't use the dark arts, Morgana. You are just as powerful without it." His hand settled down on top of mine, snuffing out my magic flame.

"How did you do that? I thought I was the only one who could put out the flame if I made it."

Merlin grinned and took his hand off mine. The flame latched onto his palm as he raised it, amazingly making the fire burn downward as if down was up. It licked across his palm, grabbing towards the bed, but he held his hand steady.

"You stole my fire," I laughed.

He chuckled, too, then set his hand down on mine again, returning the harmless flame. It produced some heat but didn't burn like a fire.

I closed my hand around it, putting out the flame, then my eyes locked on Merlin's. "Why shouldn't I use Dark Arts? I've memorized all the words."

"All of them?" Merlin asked.

I frowned. "Even the ones I will never use. I wanted to make sure I knew them all in case I lost the book." Which I had when I raced from Avalon. I had left it behind in the rubble along with the knife I had taken from Paxton's body. Pieces of me were scattered across the country. I was almost glad to be leaving when I thought about it.

"There is a price to some magic, Morgana. The cost can be steep."

He was speaking in riddles. I squinted at him from way too close. "What price?"

"One you may not want to pay. Just try to use Minerva's, or the magic you were born with. Ask the world to help you with humility. It will respond."

I bit my lip. Humility? I didn't owe the world humility, but I nodded. I could try.

Merlin grinned and leaned forward, kissing my forehead as if I was still a small child, but his warm breath washed over my face, sending a tingle through my stomach.

"Make fire with your born magic, Morgana."

I held out my hand and thought about being humble. "Fire," I said. A small spark burst from my palm, but it didn't hold fire. I bit my lip and looked back at Merlin.

"It's okay, you haven't used it in a long time. Try again. Think of your mother's magic, how you requested help, and she gave it to you."

I thought back to the words my mother had whispered in my ear. *I am not worthy*. The feeling that the words were a lie sobered me, but I pressed on. I needed humility to use the magic I was born with. "Fire," I whispered

A flame flickered to life with the soft smell of cottonwood. Merlin's grin stretched into a brilliant smile.

"I knew you could do it. You will be a powerful sorceress even without that dark magic. Just give it time and patience."

I nodded, watching his face through the flames.

Merlin's hand snuck around the fire and pushed a loose strand of my hair behind my ear. I gasped at the feeling of his fingers brushing my skin and quickly closed my hand, extinguishing the flames and sending us into the dim light.

Merlin chuckled and whispered into his hand, creating a ball of light that hovered above us.

"Your turn to tell me a story," he said, dropping his head onto the pillow and watching me with the sea-blue eyes.

I thought about telling him about Paxton, but I still wasn't sure I could tell the story without tears, so instead I told him the story of the old woman in the attic.

About how she taught me to read and gave me the book of dark arts.

Merlin listened carefully until I finished the story at the part where Copper and I raced away from the convent. Then he watched me for a long moment as if he wanted to ask a question but wasn't sure how to word it. His mouth opened and closed a few times before he finally found words.

"What was the old woman's name?"

"Margarette," I said, suddenly nervous.

Merlin didn't ask any other questions; he just sighed and closed his eyes. "I'm glad they didn't murder you."

I laughed. "Me, too."

We lapsed into silence and I watched Merlin's closed eyelids as his eyes moved about beneath them. I wasn't sure if he was asleep or just dozing, but I dared not move. I rarely had the opportunity to study his features and quite enjoyed tracing them with my eyes.

His eyebrows were curved perfectly above his eyes, his lashes longer than a typical man's and dark as they lay across his cheek. His high cheekbones gave his face a strong and angled look that wasn't softened by his typical mischievous look when he was asleep. I wanted to reach out and touch his tousled hair that had a light wave, the strands thick, but appearing soft.

"Are you staring at me, Morgana?" he asked, not opening his eyes.

"No," I lied, falling on my back and staring at the water-stained ceiling.

His chuckle drifted off, as did I, still tired from so much travel.

CHAPTER TWENTY-SIX

I woke up with a loud rumble in my stomach.

A chuckle echoed through the tiny room and I rolled over to look at Merlin, who was sitting on the foot of the bed reading a book.

"What?" I asked.

"We forgot to have dinner, and your stomach is protesting."

"Well, we'd better not forget breakfast." I righted myself and straightened my clothes, pulling the long braid out of my hair to let it fall free. It was too cramped in the small room to fuss with my hair much and it would only be another day before we made it to the Isle of Man. I could deal with the messy hair until then.

Merlin grabbed a floppy hat from his saddlebag and plopped it on his head, pulling it down low over his eyes.

"Is that your disguise?" I asked laughing.

"I think it will work if I don't bump into my old friend."

"Will we be there tonight?" I asked, hoping we didn't have to sleep in the cramped room again, even though the previous evening spent talking with Merlin had been a treat.

"Perhaps, but more likely we will arrive in the early hours of the morning."

"What's it like there?" My fingers untangled the knots that had crept into my hair as I watched Merlin's face in the low light.

"It's mostly wilderness. A few small towns dot the shore, but once you move farther in, it's all old-growth trees of dense forest." He paused, his eyes glittering. "Unless you know what you're doing. Then you can find a whole world that isn't quite like this one."

"I can't wait to see it," I said, tying off the end of my braid.

"I can't wait to show it to you." Merlin grinned, and butterflies tumbled in my stomach. "Come on, let's see if we can sneak past my old friend and get some food."

I rose and Merlin held out his arm like a gentleman. I slipped my hand into the crook of his arm and let him lead me out the door and though the narrow alleys of the ship.

"Could we stop and check on the horses?" I asked before we got too far.

"Sure," Merlin grinned and led me down a different corridor to a ladder that dropped straight down. "After you."

I let go of his arm, and grabbed hold of the ladder, stepping down carefully so I didn't trip on my skirt. At the bottom a familiar nicker greeted me.

"Hey, Copper," I said, leaving the ladder and passing the other horses to greet him. He was tied to the ropes that crossed the ship still and his feeder was full of fresh hay and a bucket of water sloshed gently beside him with every movement of the ship. He pressed his forehead into my stomach and then scratched his face on me for a moment before going back to his hay and touching his nose to Sara's beside him. She pinned her ears and grabbed a big mouthful of hay, chewing angrily.

Merlin caught up to me and slicked his hand down Sara's neck. "They've been having a nice vacation, eating to their heart's content." he turned back to his mare. "What are you so grumpy about, then?"

I laughed. "Copper is definitely enjoying his downtime. Sara looks annoyed though."

Merlin chuckled. "She always looks like that in the presence of other horses. Sorry, Copper. She is really a human in a horse's body."

Copper snorted and took a sip of his water.

"You ready to go back up?" Merlin asked.

"Sure," I said, just as a deep voice boomed behind me.

"You weren't going to avoid me this whole trip, were you?"

I spun on my heel and ran forward wrapping myself around Jag's thick chest. "Never!" I shouted, muffled by his clothes as his arms wrapped around me.

Jag laughed a deep sound that echoed through his chest where I pressed my ear. "It's good to see you all grown up, my little Morgana."

I looked up at him. "How have you been? And Lady Ethel?"

"Good, excellent actually. We have been blessed with three healthy children. She waits on the mainland for me."

"That's so great." I hugged him again and his thick arms reminded me of the feeling of being tiny. Too young and alone but having a friend in the big gruff man. He was the one to introduce me to Merlin, I recalled. His final gift to me.

"We are going up to breakfast, do you want to join us?"

I glanced back at Merlin and his face wore a frown. I didn't understand why, but before I could ask, Jag spoke again.

"Not this time. Perhaps I'll meet you for supper. I have some work to do here before I will have time to eat. But you two enjoy yourselves as much as you can with the sailor's rations."

"Thank you," Merlin said, taking my hand.

Jag's eyes widened for a second at the sight of Merlin holding my hand, then he grinned.

"I'll see you later, then," I said softly, wishing I had more time with Jag.

We parted and Merlin led me back to the ladder. "Why didn't you want to eat with him?"

"It's nothing. I just wanted to talk to you."

"Oh, all right," I said, climbing the ladder quickly. The memory of Jag scooping me off the ladder in the stable rushed back to my mind and I couldn't help the grin that took over. It would be nice to talk to him again and find out about his children. It was as if the memories had never been erased now. I could recall them so easily.

I waited at the top of the ladder for Merlin, who rose in swift, exact movements. The muscles of his arms bulged, pulling him higher. He looked up at me as he reached the top and I took a step back, lifting my eyes from his muscles, suddenly nervous at having been caught staring. His face morphed into the wicked grin, but he didn't say anything, and I was thankful. Embarrassment still coursed through my veins, heating my cheeks.

Merlin took my arm in his as we walked through the deck towards the stairs that would take us up to the top deck and the dining area. I was just about to climb the final ladder when a shout rang out and the ship shook as though we had run aground. I stumbled back, caught up by Merlin's strong arms.

"What was that?" I asked.

The ship shook again, and many screams rang out from all over the ship. Merlin steadied me on my feet and flew up the ladder faster than I had ever seen anyone move. I climbed up after him, but he had already moved beyond the top when I stepped out onto the top deck.

As I straightened, I came face to face with a barbarian of a man. His hair was a mess of knots and his beard was long and ragged. He yelled something in a language I didn't understand and his hand, wielding a sword came down towards me.

"Bebeorgan," I screamed.

Protect.

His blade stopped mere inches from me. I stared at him, still in shock as his eyes grew round and he spoke again, saying words I didn't know, but I glanced down at his chest barring the same tattoo as Paxton had. He was a Saxon. Of course, he knew what *Bebeorgan* meant as I knew now the words were in his language, but the shocked look on his face still said he had never come across this magic before.

While we were still staring at each other, this almost reverent look came over his face. We were two solitary figures in a world of chaos. The top deck was full of men fighting, swords clanging and screams of pain. But I and this one lone Saxon were frozen like rocks in the middle of a river.

I blinked and the tip of a sword appeared from the centre of the Saxon's chest. His eyes grew wide and then faded as he collapsed to the planks.

"Come on!" Merlin yelled from right behind where the Saxon had stood, his sword bloody in his hand and blood spraying harsh red across his face. "We have to save the ship. It's going down."

That snapped me out of my shock. I followed him for a few steps before I heard a horse scream.

"I have to save Copper!" I yelled over the noise and turned, racing back to the ladder.

"Morgana! I need your help!" Merlin said from behind me, but I didn't slow. I nearly fell down the ladder, then raced past men with swords dressed in Roman army uniforms. Of course, Commander Artorius' men would fight off the invaders. But if the ship was going down, I needed to save Copper. I wouldn't let him down again. That was all I could think about as I tripped over my skirt, falling to my knees and cutting my palms on the rough planks. I scrambled upright and continued toward the lower deck. My feet pounding along faster than my heart racing in my ears.

The screams were muffled by the planks above my head, but the thumps of men falling were loud enough.

I blocked it all out. I had no time to think about the commander or even Merlin. He had magic; I was sure he would be fine, and the commander and Jag were strong soldiers. But Copper was tied to a rope. He would drown if the ship went down.

I careened around the last corner and ran straight into Jag.

"Whoa! Morgana. Return to your cabin, you will be safe there until the fighting is over." He ran off before

I could tell him that the ship was going down. I continued to the ladder, swinging my legs over the side and scrambling down it as quickly as I could.

I jumped the last few rungs and landed in a puddle. I looked down, surprised to find water there, then looked around and discovered the whole floor of the boat was underwater. The horses splashed and pranced, anxious. Then I found the source. A large crack in the wall of the hull that was letting in the water much faster than anyone could bucket it out.

The ship was going down, and that was the moment I remembered we were in the middle of the ocean, days from shore.

CHAPTER TWENTY-SEVEN

I splashed through the water as it grew deeper, already over the height of my boots, and raced to Copper. I struggled to undo his halter from the rope they tied the horses to. The horses were all anxious now, dancing in the cold ocean water that grew higher and higher with each second.

"Hold still!" I yelled, but it was no use. My fingers fumbled, but finally loosed the knot and went to work on Sara's. If I'd had a blade, I would have cut them all free, but as it was it took so long to just untie Copper and Sara that the water was above my knees. The yelling from the top deck was fading, I prayed that Merlin was safe, but had no time. I had to find a way out of the ship before it sunk with us inside.

I grabbed Copper's mane and swung up onto his back, still holding Sara's lead. The other horses danced and yanked back at their ties as we moved through the aisle toward the big door that had been opened to let the horses in when the boat was docked.

There was no ramp leading up to it, but that soon wouldn't matter as the water grew deeper around us. The shouting above me grew louder, and I wasn't sure if that was a good sign. It didn't matter. The ship we were on was sinking fast. The water was already at Copper's sides, my feet hanging in the water.

Sara bounded along behind us, the water splashing up with each stride until her hooves no longer reached the floor and she began to swim. Copper was only a few inches taller, but he began to swim too. The amazing feeling of floating was only disturbed by the fact that the boat began to tip. The rest of the horses began to panic, thrashing around, some disappearing below the water behind us and I turned back to face the wall of the boat.

As the big door lowered towards the water, Copper's legs thrust beneath the surface. The ceiling was getting closer to my head as the water rose.

"Gypung," I screamed.

Open.

The boat screamed and groaned but the door flung open, shards of wood flew in every direction and a moment later the water rushed in unhindered, throwing me from Copper's back and pulling me under the water.

My mouth opened in a scream that was cut off by the weight of ice-cold water pushing me under. I spun, trying to orient myself in the dark murk. It was impossible. I kicked my feet, only to become tangled in some ropes and come face to face with a horse who had already perished.

The shock caused me to gasp and water filled my lungs, clouding my mind and increasing my panic. I needed oxygen. I kicked again one last determined time, but the water just went on forever. My head felt heavy, and I wanted to close my eyes and just stop.

Everything slowed down. The water caressed me, hanging me in an endless moment of peace and quiet. I floated in the silent world, painless and unending.

A voice whispered in the back of my mind. "You must be strong, Morgana." It was my mother's words from the last time I saw her. Her voice was serious and so determined.

Euphoria rushed in, replacing the quiet surrender. My spine straightened and my chin raised as the now familiar feeling of the Dark Arts power filled me. I no longer needed air. I knew I would live but had to get out of the boat.

The word '*Blot*' came to my mind. It was a word from the back of the book that I knew meant sacrifice. I mouthed the word and felt the rush of power. I didn't know how it fit in this situation until the boat began to fall apart and rising pressure rushed me toward the surface faster than I could swim.

My head breached the surface, and I gasped, coughing up water and replacing it with air. My spine was still tingling with the pressure of the magic and I knew it wasn't done. There was a smaller boat beside where the ship had been. It was crawling with Saxons. They had swords raised in victory and were yelling. Celebrating, I realized, the victory against the Roman army they had vanquished.

My power boiled beneath my skin as another word of magic slipped from my lips. One that I knew too well.

"Abrecan," I said.

Destroy.

The boat the Saxon warriors stood upon splintered into a million pieces. Shards of wood pierced the men as they fell into the water, staining the water red. The wreckage was expanding, pieces of wood and bodies floating all around me.

My magic drained away, leaving me weak and tired.

"Copper!" I yelled. Spinning around, trying to see past the floating pieces. "Copper!"

A strangled nicker reached my ears from far away. I spun towards the sound and began to swim. My years living by the sea had made me a strong swimmer, but my skirt slowed me with its weight. I reached down and tore it away; swimming in just my underthings was easier. My tiger skin was lost, too, but I didn't need it now; I needed my horse and Merlin. I flipped over several bodies I came across, but none were Merlin.

When I reached Copper, I swung onto his back. I couldn't think straight, but once I was settled on Copper, I felt as if I was safe. Stupid. I was in the middle of the ocean without a boat, but Copper's warm comfort soothed the fear and pain.

From his back, I had a higher view of the water around me and called out to Merlin.

I got no reply, except for the nicker of Sara who swam up beside us.

I grasped her lead from the water, and she peddled along. "Where is your master?" I asked her.

She turned her head and began to swim away, pulling at her lead as if she knew which way to go. I nudged Copper's side to get him to go that direction. We swam for several minutes, passing men who had been killed or drowned until Sara stopped beside Merlin's still form. He floated face down. I launched myself off Copper's back, swimming the last of the distance to the wizard's side, and flipped him onto his back. His hair fanned around him like a halo, but his skin was the pale white of death. His lips were blue and chest still. A sob tore from me before I had time to even take in his full appearance.

Before the first tear could fall, power welled, stronger than before. My back cracked and my body rose out of the water. I was all-powerful. I was the most powerful sorceress in the world, and nothing would stop me from getting my way. I wanted the wizard to live and I would not be denied.

Power screamed through me as a word slammed into my mind.

"Gelibban," I shouted, peering down at the water and Merlin's still form, moved only by the gentle waves that rocked the water.

Merlin's skin grew pink, and he coughed, exploding into movement. His arms flailed and his head disappeared below the water for a moment before he breached the surface. He vomited water and gasped a few more times as I sunk slowly back into the water beside him. I could hardly breathe I was so exhausted. But Merlin's eyes rolled back in his head and I knew he would drown again if I didn't get him to safety.

I dragged him through the water toward Sara, his body trembling, but breath going in and out in a steady rhythm. I pressed him onto Sara's back, once he was there, and used Sara's lead rope and halter to secure him to her, his head resting on her neck, above the water.

I could hardly move my arms or legs to keep myself afloat as I climbed back onto Copper's back and collapsed against his neck.

The horses began to swim. I had no idea where they were headed, but I trusted Copper to get us out of the mess. Slowly the debris dispersed, and I lay my head down on Copper's neck. We bobbed in the water, beneath the stark blue sky and I was lulled as the sound of my breathing was the only sound. The air was much colder than the water and I huddled low in the water, hoping I didn't freeze.

I fought my eyes that wanted to close, but the strength had left me. The images of the dead bodies clung to my mind, tormenting me, but I couldn't stop sleep from taking over, and eventually, the world went back.

CHAPTER TWENTY-EIGHT

I woke to Copper's loud neigh, his body shaking beneath me. The sun was past its highest point and making its descent in the sky now.

I sat up and looked around, hopeful that land was somewhere in sight, but all I found was blue. I glanced behind me, just as Sara's head struggled back above the water.

"Oh, no!" I cried. "Sara, swim!"

The whites of her eyes were wide. She was terrified and her thrashing was growing weaker. I climbed off of Copper and swam to her side. Then pulled at the knots I had tied to keep Merlin on her back and dragged his dead weight from her.

I tried to call forward some magic, but I was too tired, and no power came. No magic word that would save the grey mare. Nothing.

She was too weak; it was no use, she was sinking. "I'm sorry," I whispered to her, patting her forehead.

She was a good mare. A strong warrior who had swum all this time, but the distance was too far to expect her to make it. Copper was magic; I was beginning to think he could swim all day and night and never tire. But Sara was mortal. She was not made to swim for hours and hours.

If we made it to land, Merlin would mourn her, and from the way Copper was swimming in circles around the mare, I knew he would miss her, too.

Despite Copper's agitation and relentless nudges, Sara was getting lower and lower in the water. Her movements were slowing, and her gasping breaths were fractions away from taking in water.

Just as Sara seemed to give up and slow to a stop, a spark flew out of the necklace Copper still wore tied in his mane. The one my mother had given me. I was too exhausted to be amazed, but more sparks came from the necklace until they were falling all over the grey mare. Her movements smoothed out and her strokes came easier as she began to swim with renewed strength.

Copper nickered at her and pressed his nose to her neck. She nickered in return and nudged him back.

Tears sprung to my eyes, and I rolled Merlin's still prone form onto Sara's back again. I wasn't sure how much longer she would last, but my hope was renewed that we would all get to shore.

With Merlin secured, I climbed back onto Copper and the horses moved gracefully through the water. My head fell back to Copper's neck, and I rested as the water washed past me, keeping my eyes on the grey mare and wizard. Merlin's breaths came slow and steady, but his eyes still hadn't opened. His color was good, a bit red thanks to the sunny day. We would surely have burnt skin if we made it to shore. When we made it to shore. I would keep hope.

My fingers were blue, and the cold seemed to rip through my skin as I hunkered below the lapping water.

I tried to work out how long it would take, but I had no idea how fast the boat could travel compared to a horse swimming.

I let my mind wander to the past, just to escape the pain of the cold and the reality of what I had done. My mother. I remembered the soft scent of orange blossoms that lingered even after she had left a room. Her soft touch on my cheek and her smile as she spoke to me.

I closed my eyes and could almost feel her gentle hands smoothing my hair and whispering stories to me. Stories of my father's bravery and of her life when she was a child. The tale of how she met my father in a local village when he was there selling a cow and she was there selling berries at a small stand. The memories of swimming with my sister were easy to fall into when I was in the water. Splashing and running together in the warmth of long summer days.

Copper never faltered. His legs moved effortlessly in long powerful strokes. His nicker pulled me back from my memories, and I sat up, stretching out my legs. I glanced around and thought I saw something off in the distance. At first, I thought my mind was playing tricks on me, or the fading daylight was making an optical illusion. But the longer we swam, the clearer the horizon looked and the more it looked like trees.

"Is that land?" I asked, my throat parched and voice scratchy. Nobody could answer me since Merlin was still unconscious, and the horses obviously couldn't speak.

I stared at Merlin for a while, willing him to wake up. Was the land Isle of Man? I couldn't tell, but the relief of seeing the land was like a weight lifted off me.

We could find help there, water and food. I was so thirsty, surrounded by water, but none that I could drink. Father had warned me when I was young not to drink the ocean water. He said it wouldn't quench my thirst, only make me want to drink more. So, I had been careful, even under the midday sun, not to drink it. It lapped at my thighs as Copper continued on, swimming as if he could keep going all day. Sara, too, looked like she could keep going, but I could tell the moment she spotted the horizon. Her ears perked up and the soft rumble of a nicker came from her pink flared nostrils. Her long silver mane fanned around her and shone in the fading sunlight.

"We are almost there, Merlin. We are going to make it," I said, my voice wavering in excitement.

I wasn't sure how the horses had made it there so quickly, but I was willing to bet magic had something to do with it. Magic always seemed to find a way.

The horses were both in a race now. The water splashed and sloshed between them as they drew nearer to the shore. With the sun finally set, the moon reflected off the water, giving it an eerie glow that twinkled over the ripples and waves. The gentle sloshing sound was drowned out by the calls of seabirds as we approached the island. Huge cliffs circled the shore, trees crowded together at the top making it look like a dark crown on the ocean.

An acrid smell slammed into us like a wall. The horses all stopped and tried to paddle back from the wicked scent. I covered my nose, but the smell burned my mouth and throat. Suddenly the horses were racing away from the island, but we had nowhere else to go.

"No, turn back, Copper. We have no choice!" A coughing fit took over and I heaved into the ocean but grabbed onto his mane and used my legs to direct him back around. I prayed it was just a temporary smell because I wouldn't be able to stand it long, but we had to try.

"Copper!" I yelled, and he finally slowed and turned back towards the island. The smell had dissipated, but the horses were not in a hurry to return to that foul smell.

They bobbed along at a sedate, cautious pace, while I scanned the water and shore, trying to decide if the smell had come from a decaying creature. The horses turned to swim along the shore instead of towards it. If there was something dead on the beach, we could avoid it that way, but I didn't see anything capable of making such a horrible smell.

After a few minutes, I encouraged Copper to try to reach the shore again. "This time, don't stop," I whispered to him and he strained his muscles beneath me but swam towards the sandy beach.

The foul smell returned, and I covered my nose again, wishing I could do the same for Copper and Sara, but they struggled forward, racing now against the smell of rot. The scent intensified until my eyes were tearing and burning and a word of power came to my mind like a blade to my hand.

"Belucan," I shouted.

Stop.

It was a strange word to use in this situation, but immediately the scent lifted, and the horses snorted. I sighed, and we made our way toward the shore.

I tried to think of the implications of the word stop making the smell stop. Perhaps someone of magic had made the smell to keep people away. But it seemed like a lot of trouble to go to just to keep people away from an island in the middle of the ocean. I couldn't see how large it was in the darkness, but Merlin hadn't made it sound large or valuable, except for the fact there was another world somehow attached to it. Magic worked in mysterious ways and if someone had made that smell as a deterrent, I prayed there wasn't more in store for me.

"Merlin," I called, shaking his shoulder. He was still breathing but hadn't woken even in that foul odour. I wondered if he would ever wake. He didn't appear to have any injuries, so I wasn't sure why he was unconscious in the first place.

If there were magic users on the island, perhaps one of them could help Merlin. No magic came to me as I considered his prone form, so I assumed I couldn't help him. I struggled to even think of a word that would help when just a few minutes before the word to solve the smelly problem had come to me like magic.

I grinned at that thought. Imagine that. A magic word coming to me like magic.

I had no more time to think about it, though, as Copper's hooves touched bottom and he switched from swimming to walking. The feeling of his legs on the earth was foreign after so long at sea. My body resented the movement and my head spun. Copper and Sara seemed to feel the same strangeness as they staggered towed the sandy beach.

"Good job, Copper," I said stroking his neck. He arched his neck and began prancing before I even felt the magic rising within me. I was exhausted, but magic surged, making me feel as though I was invincible. I was the queen of the new land we tread upon.

Even Sara got in on the action, her owner draped across her back. Her neck and tail rose, making her movements exaggerated and animated. The feeling didn't last long though. As soon as it rose, it began to fade. Taking the last of my energy with it. I slumped forward and then tipped off Copper's back as we reached the sandy beach.

I broke my fall, but still ended up face down in the soft sand, still warm from the sun's rays. My body convulsed in shivers as the wind whipped across my wet skin.

Copper's heavy grunt told me he had collapsed behind me and I turned my head in time to see Sara slowly lower herself to the beach sand, too, her eyes sliding closed and chin resting heaving in the soft sand. Between them, I was protected from the wind at least.

"Thank you," I whispered to her, my eyes fixed on Merlin. I didn't know where I was, but I knew as long as Merlin was there, I was home.

CHAPTER TWENTY-NINE

My eyes opened to find the sun peeking over the horizon. My mouth was dry, and sand had crept in while I slept, making my teeth crunch as the grains churned around my mouth. I pushed myself up and wiped the side of my face, then tried to find a part of my shirt that was clean to wipe my mouth on, but there was no part of my clothes I wanted anywhere near my mouth. Hopefully, I could find a stream somewhere or even a puddle. I glanced around and found Sara, still carrying Merlin's prone form, munching on the leaves of some trees growing out of the rocky wall of the cliffs. Copper stood beside her, uninterested in the green nibblets.

I rose and crossed to them, wishing I hadn't tossed my skirt now that I was on dry land. My underwear was hardly suitable to walk through the dense forest above us. If we could even find a way up there.

I approached Sara first, ensuring Merlin was balanced on her back and re-tied the ropes holding him in place while the mare stood silently, still as a statue.

I recalled Merlin's story of the Sheik and his brave mare. Merlin was draped across her shoulder, much as I imagined the Sheik had been, returning to his village bloody and already dead. I checked over Merlin again, running my hands through his hair that had dried overnight and checking beneath his coat. There were still no injuries. His condition would remain a mystery until he finally rose from his unconscious state.

"Well, should we find a way up there?" I asked the horses. I peered up, blocking the sun from my eyes. The rock face was too steep to climb, hopefully, we could circle the island and find a way up. If people lived there, they had to have a way up.

I walked along, happy to use my own legs, as Copper and Sara followed behind. My bare feet squished through the warm sand. It was peaceful here. The gulls called, and the waves lapped gently, but otherwise, it was silent. Copper's whiskers brushed against my arm and I reached over, mindlessly stroking his cheek and up behind his ears. His coat was crisp from the saltwater, and sand blew out as I rubbed him. The further we walked the eerier the wildness of the island seemed. Merlin had said that many people lived in the magic that hovered on or over the island.

The cliff didn't seem to be getting any shorter if anything it was higher here. I began to worry I was walking the wrong way and would end up circling the whole island before I found a way up.

My legs grew tired quickly as the lack of food and water began to weigh me down. The beach stretched on for miles, and though the sun was warm the constant icy wind was freezing on my bare legs.

Finally, I came to a small trickle of water that ran down the side of the cliff. It was barely more than a drop, but I stopped and pressed my lip to the hard stone, slurping up the dribble of water as if it were nectar. It was cool and fresh, sliding down my parched throat. I drank for several minutes, letting the water trickle straight into my gut then gathered a bit in the palm of my hand and pressed the few measly drops to Merlin's lips. Repeating the action a few more times didn't seem to make any difference. Any water I got in his mouth, just ran out again. I was getting cold standing in one place, but the sun was still up, so I traveled further down the coast, hoping to find a cave or somewhere I could rest that wasn't out in the open. The day stretched on. It felt as if I should have circled the island already, but the shore just stretched on until eventually the beach seemed to narrow. The water getting closer to the solid rock wall.

"This is probably not good, Copper," I said to break the silence that had been hanging over us for hours. My voice was still harsh and rough.

I stopped and looked up at the Cliff again, knowing there had to be a way up. I felt a small spark of magic rise inside me and waited to see if a magic word would come from somewhere deep inside, something that would get us to the top of the stupid cliffs. It was at the tip of my tongue; I was reaching through my mind trying to find it when I heard a voice.

"Who are you?"

I looked all around; there was none on the beach in either direction.

"Look up!" the voice said.

There at the top of the cliff, a woman stood, I couldn't make out her features, but her hair was magnificently blonde. Lighter than Paxton's had been. She wore a band of material that circled her body, leaving her arms free beneath an animal skin that she wore draped off one shoulder. She oozed elegance, something I had never had but had coveted in women whenever I saw it.

"My name is Morgana, and this is Merlin!" I shouted back.

In a flash, the woman stood before me. I jumped back and so did the horses, startled at her sudden appearance.

"What's happened?" her hands moved over Merlin's face as if she knew him. "What happened?" she repeated, her eyes darting to me with an accusation.

"Our ship was attacked. Everyone died." The ratchet of pain stung through my chest at saying it out loud. I had sacrificed everyone who may have still been alive to get out of that ship. It hadn't occurred to me until this morning what the sacrifice had been, but now that I knew, I was teetering on the edge of insanity.

Commander and Jag had both been among the casualties. I had no more strength to deny it. Now that we had been found by someone who obviously used magic, and as I started to feel a little like everything would be okay, the walls I had put up to keep the devastation out of my mind crumbled.

A tear streaked my face and the strange woman saw it, her stance softening.

"You did well to get Merlin here and two horses..." she trailed off, her eyes roaming over Copper. "Well, one horse and another, of sorts."

I couldn't help but notice the way her hand cupped Merlin's face, nor the rise of jealousy that stung at me.

"You'll be alright now, love," she whispered to Merlin. "Just hang on a bit longer and we will get you home where you belong."

Rage threatened to overcome me. She shouldn't be so familiar with him. Merlin was mine! Wait, what? I took a deep breath and let it out slowly. Merlin wasn't mine. We were just friends from long ago. I needed to keep myself in check or I wouldn't have any help for Merlin or myself.

"Is there someone who can help him? I don't know what's wrong."

The beautiful woman stroked Sara's head, murmuring words to her, then turned to look at me. "He used too much magic, there is a price for everything. A check and balance." She took in my appearance, and I was suddenly self-conscious of my lack of a skirt, but I stood and let her eyes appraise me. "You have a lot of wild magic."

That was all she said before she turned and began walking down the beach, Sara followed her and Copper followed Sara, so I jogged to catch up.

"Here we are," she said, waving her arm. Suddenly the stone wall disappeared, displaying instead a grassy hill that would be easy to climb.

"Why do you keep this hidden?" I asked, stepping barefoot onto the lush green grass. It felt like heaven beneath my tired feet.

"Because it is the road to the Mannin. And only the most powerful of sorceresses and wizards are allowed to dwell in this place. Only those who control the world's magic with the palm of their hands." Her eyes inspected me again, their green the same shade as that of the grass and foliage that surrounded the path. "I suspect Merlin was bringing you here for a very good reason."

She turned her head back, and I had more than enough to think about as we tracked up the hill. The trees waved gently in the subtle breeze and the higher we climbed the warmer the weather. My fingers lost the numb chill that had been plaguing them since I climbed out of the ocean, and the colour in Merlin's cheeks returned.

I wanted to cup his face as the strange woman had done. I wanted to reach out and hold his hand. We were back where he wanted to be, or where he wanted me to be. Any way you looked at it we had made it, despite all the terror on the ocean, despite swimming countless miles… Here we were.

We crested the hill finally and my eyes grew wide, amazed at the beautiful world below.

"Whoa," I said.

"Remarkable, isn't it?" The woman said, skipping forward towards the circle of small houses below. "Welcome to Mannin, Morgana Le Fay!"

I was struck, stunned for a long moment staring at the picturesque beauty before it occurred to me… I hadn't given her my full name.